PENGUIN BOOKS

*Editor: Julian Symons*

CANDLESHOE

Michael Innes is the pseudonym of J. I. M. Stewart, who was a Student of Christ Church, Oxford, from 1949 until his retirement in 1973. He was born in 1906 and was educated at Edinburgh Academy and Oriel College, Oxford. He was lecturer in English at the University of Leeds from 1930 to 1935, and spent the succeeding ten years as Jury Professor of English in the University of Adelaide, South Australia.

He has published twelve novels and two volumes of short stories, as well as many detective stories and broadcast scripts under the pseudonym of Michael Innes. His *Eight Modern Writers* appeared in 1963 as the final volume of *The Oxford History of English Literature*. Michael Innes is married and has five children.

# Candleshoe

MICHAEL INNES

PENGUIN BOOKS

Penguin Books Ltd, Harmondsworth, Middlesex, England
Penguin Books, 625 Madison Avenue, New York, New York 10022, U.S.A.
Penguin Books Australia Ltd, Ringwood, Victoria, Australia
Penguin Books Canada Ltd, 2801 John Street, Markham, Ontario, Canada L3R 1B4
Penguin Books (N.Z.) Ltd, 182–190 Wairau Road, Auckland 10, New Zealand

—

First published by Gollancz as *Christmas at Candleshoe* 1953
Published in Penguin Books 1961
Reprinted under the present title 1978

—

—

Made and printed in Great Britain by
C. Nicholls & Company Ltd
Set in Linotype Granjon

CHRISTMAS, GERARD *(d. 1634), carver and statuary; carved funeral monuments; carver to the navy, 1614–34; designer of figures for several lord mayors' shows between 1611 and 1632.*

*The Concise Dictionary of National Biography*

# CHAPTER ONE

WE are looking at an English rural landscape on a summer afternoon. Most of us are urban folk – we come from New York and London and Birmingham and St Louis – and our principal sensation is the comfortable one of getting our money's worth. The Englishness is unchallengeable, the rurality unflawed, and the whole effect a landscape in the fullest sense of the word. This last circumstance, indeed, makes a few of us obscurely uneasy.

Delimiting the foreground, beyond a broad expanse of lawn, is a low and unassuming stone wall. Our eye lingers upon it, and we wonder why. Well, diagonally upon it falls another line – that of a small clear river flowing away into the middle distance. And it so happens that, in the picture-space we are contemplating, the one line cuts the other in a ratio which artists call golden section. Moreover the diagonal line of the river is balanced by an answering diagonal in the long slope of an adjacent hill, and we are further aware that to left and right, just comfortably within our peripheral vision, grove nods to grove and wood advances upon wood as in the sinuous symmetry of some sophisticated dance. Knowing that nature never contrives precisely such effects, we realize that the river has been diverted, the hill manufactured, and the circumambient forest persuaded to approach and take up a station in consonance with the general effect. We are studying a work of art.

More, we are the heirs of all the ages. Whate'er Lorraine light-touched with softening hue, or savage Rosa dashed, or learned Poussin drew has gone to build up this picture; the Gothic is present in a durably constructed ruin partly screened by Druidic oaks; and across the lawn stretches the shadow of an intricate and enormous object, presently to be explored, which could never have been thought of but for the lucidity of Greece and the grandeur of Rome. If in the course of the past few weeks we have been doing things in a really big way – perambulating, perhaps, the picture-galleries of the continent, pausing for appropriate minutes before three-starred canvasses, and refraining from any culpable lingering before inferior productions – if we have been doing this sort of thing we may feel that some optical trick is now being played on us; that effects properly to be contrived as a mild illusion upon a demonstrably flat surface have here been made ingeniously stereoscopic; and that by pressing a button or removing a pair of cunningly contrived spectacles we shall cause all the mass and roundedness to vanish, and be looking at nothing more out-of-the-way than a good canvas by Richard Wilson.

But there is the sky. Small clouds are actually moving across it, and light and shade play over the scene. On the lawn, beyond the farthest tip of the great still shadow, something – a further shadow – flutters. We turn, craning our necks upwards. High above the vast complicated building flies a small complicated flag. As the breeze catches it and flattens it out it becomes – we vaguely conjecture – generously and awesomely informative. If we knew a griffin from a wyvern, and could name when we saw them gules three pales vair and a chief gold, this fluttering scrap might largely if somewhat imaginatively instruct us in a substantial corner of English history. As it is, we may be content with the thing's simpler advertisement. The Marquess of Scattergood is in residence at Benison Court.

Lord Scattergood is entertaining guests. Groups of them are on the lawn with us now, and others are strolling in remoter parts of the gardens. The *jet d'eau* has been turned on and evokes admiration; the water-steps – so charmingly reproduced in miniature at Chatsworth – are agreeably cool; the Neptune fountain, with its circling and spouting dolphins and its diving Nereid, is accounted a marvellous toy. The palm houses and orangeries please some; others in two stately gondolas venture upon the surface of the south lake; smaller parties explore the temple of Artemis, the hermit's grotto (disused), the ice-house, the sixth marquess's improved milking-parlour in the Chinese taste. Most however are indoors, and so too is Lord Scattergood himself. The state apartments are open, and large numbers move about in them. Lord Scattergood, in the middle of a small group (thus highly if somewhat randomly privileged), dominates the octagon room, full of affability. He had good reason to be delighted. It is a peak hour and the place is doing well. In the great courtyard the turnstiles never cease to click, and the park is alive with *chars-à-bancs*, like enormous beeves at pasture. Everybody has paid either three shillings for the house, or half-a-crown for the gardens, or five shillings for both.

Lord Scattergood feels, very properly, that he owes rather more to all these people than if they had paid nothing at all. So he leads his group around and is prodigal of information. Much of it is inaccurate, since it has been Lord Scattergood's habit to take his possessions for granted and revere them less in detail than in the mass. Even his elderly younger son, Lord Arthur Spendlove, who is also acting as cicerone, gets fewer of the dates wrong and is less apt to muddle the rebuildings and restorings and royal visits. But then one cannot have everything, even for five shillings. It is something to be done the honours of Benison by a Spendlove, and particularly by a Marquess of Scattergood himself. And Lord Scattergood's manners are so nice that we can feel quite at home. It is true that the elder statesmen who stroll up and down in a detached way through these large vistas are detectives.

But they would be here, just the same, if Lord Scattergood was giving a party strictly confined within the limits of the peerage. Were he giving a large-scale family party, it would be his impulse to have them doubled. But this is something you would never guess as you look at him. He has all the appearance of reposing in utter confidence within his own inviolable caste. His present affability has its first and cardinal condition in that.

'I ought to begin, you know, by explaining that my people have lived here at Benison for quite a long time. I don't mean, of course, that the place is frightfully old. As you can see for yourselves, it quite definitely isn't. From the look of it' – and at this Lord Scattergood glances about him with all the appearance of a freshly appraising eye – 'from the look of it, I should say it was run up long after Queen Elizabeth and Shakespeare and Cromwell and all that thoroughly historical crowd. It's no good coming to Benison for the feel of that sort of thing. In Scotland I have a place called Corbies – my eldest boy lives there at present – where you get much more of all that. Dungeons, I mean, and a drawbridge, and deuced primitive drains.'

'Would your family ghost be there?'

It is an American lady who in all boldness and innocence asks this question. There is a ripple of embarrassed laughter. A small man clutching a child in either hand – he is a greengrocer from Nottingham – blushes painfully: his delicacy is outraged. But Lord Scattergood has had this one before and is delighted. 'Certainly. The family ghost has never come down here, I am glad to say. Not that he is in any way really tiresome. Only' – something new and pleasing flashes into Lord Scattergood's head – 'only whenever he appears he is accompanied by a skirl of bagpipes – and that, of course, can be disturbing in the middle of the night. But I was remarking that one doesn't come to Benison, don't you know, for the medieval side of things. The Henrys, and all that. When I was a lad my father packed me off to a big school near Windsor – and there, if you understand me, there is much more that takes you back to chainmail, and the Crusades, and those Wars of the Roses in which so many people you meet got badly cut up. But here at Benison we are seventeenth and eighteenth century, and we have got along in a very orderly way on the whole. Those carvings' – and Lord Scattergood abruptly extends a finely tapering finger as he makes this transition from the general to the particular – 'those carvings above the doorway are by a fellow called Grinling Gibbons. Or was it Edward Gibbon? I remember my grandmother telling me they were both little men who came down and worked here from time to time.'

Lord Scattergood, conscious of being a shade vague, pauses to collect himself. The little group gazes around and talks in whispers. The whispering is something they feel to be polite; it is not the issue of timidity. People are impressed but not overawed. They have just been told, it is true, that such and such paintings are by Titian and such and such by Velasquez; that here is a casket by Cellini and there a wax figure by Michelangelo. But are they not, after all, familiar with super-cinemas? And has not the cinema-screen itself conducted them in the course of historical films through palaces more gorgeous than this? Obscurely but quite confidently, the English feel that things have happened which make them, in a sense, joint-owners with the Marquess both of Benison itself and of all its treasures. They are in the same boat with Lord Scattergood; they will sink or swim together; on this sunny afternoon it is pleasant to have been invited to climb to the bridge. Their five shillings are forgotten; they are well-disposed and well-behaved guests; it will be to-morrow before some of them recall that they have peeped into a fantastically remote and still obstinately privileged world.

The Americans are different. They are keeping the full measure of their awe for the Tower of London, the crypts of the great cathedrals, the birthplace of Shakespeare in Stratford, the cradle of the Washington family at Sulgrave Manor. That the owner of Benison Court should confess the place to be of no great antiquity impresses and pleases them; they see in it the high standard of personal honour which the English aristocracy – they believe – manages to combine with the utmost of Machiavellian duplicity in the political and diplomatic sphere. At the same time a few of them are looking at their watches, and presently one of them asks the question that is in all their minds. He is a bald pale person from Buffalo, where he carries on the profession of mortician. Conceivably by way of reaction from this sombre calling, he now wears a lemon-coloured suit and an extraordinary tie – a tie as complicated as the flag now fluttering above Benison, and akin to it – we may feel – as a gesture of naïf ostentation. The mortician has a camera slung at the ready just above the bulge of his stomach, and this gives to the most prominent part of his person the appearance of a large Cyclops-face set directly upon two short legs. He swings round and faces Lord Scattergood with the camera's single staring eye. 'What', he demands, 'is the oldest thing you have here?'

The mortician is paying Lord Scattergood a compliment, is acknowledging him to be the sort of man who will take and deal with a straight question. And Lord Scattergood is once more delighted. The vocation of Edward Gibbon, although he must have learnt it when at the large school near Windsor, has long ago passed out of his head. But he knows how to answer the mortician. 'Well now, talking of that, I can show you rather a jolly thing.' On long loose limbs he strides out of the octagon room; from the back he might be a youth of twenty; the tourists puff and shuffle after him, their foothold uncertain on the great polished floors. They file between rows of portraits, a complexity of mirrors, cliffs of books; they descend a broad cold staircase hung with enormous canvases of conjectural Spendloves prancing upon badly foreshortened horses. Presently they are peering into a chill and musty gloom, while their guide fumbles for an electric switch. 'There you are. Rather fun – what?'

With a flicker and a ping a bar of fluorescent lighting has snapped on. Lord Scattergood's party takes on an unhealthy tinge and the mortician might be a piece of bad embalming. Only Lord Scattergood's own complexion is so florid as to be indestructible. He watches with amusement as his guests peer doubtfully into the great wedge-shaped space beneath the last flight of stairs. It is the corner into which, in a suburban house, one pushes the pram. And now Lord Scattergood's guests, as if they were Gullivers in a Brobdingnagian semi-detached villa, are looking at an enormous baby-carriage, elaborately painted and carved. The greengrocer's younger child becomes excited and utters cries.

'Constructed for the children of the Swedish Countess in 1722.' Lord Scattergood embarks somewhat uncertainly on an explanation of how this lady found herself a Spendlove. 'But, as you can see, it is really a sledge. She is said to have had reindeer brought over, and in winter her children went bowling about the park.'

'Did you have more snow in those days than you have now?' The American lady who inquired about the ghost has put this question with an air of much acuteness. Lord Scattergood, cheerfully accepting the character of a Methuselah, replies that the winters were decidedly more severe then than now.

Meanwhile the sledge is being a great success. It is pronounced to be cute and sweet. A young female from Sydney, who is mostly bare legs and an enormous rucksack, declares it to be dandy. The greengrocer's younger child starts shouting. Only the mortician from Buffalo remembers the motive behind this inspection. With professional deftness he applies a scraping finger-nail to a leather surface. 'I don't get this,' he says. '1722 isn't so very old. And it don't *look* old, either.'

'Ah – you misunderstood me.' Lord Scattergood glances amiably round, collecting the attention of his auditory. 'It's not the carriage itself that is at all notably old. I'm not sure that the fellow Gibbons I was mentioning didn't have a hand in it. But the sledge-runners *are* quite old – and fine pieces of timber, as you can see. Cedar wood. They came from the Middle East.'

'The Middle East?' The mortician is suspicious.

'Yes – brought back by an ancestor of mine – quite an enterprising fellow – from the top of Mount Ararat. Ship's timbers, he decided they were. And he was a sailor, so he ought to have known.'

The more mentally alert of Lord Scattergood's hearers giggle or gasp. An explanatory voice at the back, unconscious of offence, says, 'Blessed if the ol' bastard doesn't say 'e's got Noah's ruddy Ark.' The greengrocer's second child, thus hearing mention of this object of juvenile enchantment, breaks loose, rushes forward, trips, grazes a knee, and howls. The greengrocer's wife, deeply mortified, seizes the child, rights him, and is about to administer the alarming if innocuous shaking with which in England the simpler classes are accustomed to admonish their young. But Lord Scattergood is before her, whisks the child to his shoulder, and marches off with brisk talk of warm water and sticking-plaster. The greengrocer, his wife, and his elder child follow. They are really awed now. Lord Scattergood pauses until they catch up. He has forgotten his damned tourists and the turn he puts on for them. The child has casually attracted him, and for five minutes he will chat to the parents just as he would do to any of his great neighbours in the county. He believes that they will go away with the unspoken knowledge that one does not shake small children.

Autocratic and benevolent, Lord Scattergood disappears. The group remains for a moment in uncertainty, staring at the sledge. But almost at once a less exalted guide sweeps down on them and politely carries them off. Opening Benison Court to the public has proved to be a money-earner. A good deal of efficiency has been mobilized for the job.

But at Benison even quite a lot of efficiency is liable to get spread out thin. Lord Arthur Spendlove, as he leads his own party round, knows all the closets where chaos and confusion lurk. The very skeletons in the cupboards, he likes to remark, are in a sad muddle. A clever man, seemingly shiftless because profoundly at odds with his time, Lord Arthur wonders if any amount of efficiency could now make much difference. His father, briefed by some soothing old donkey in Chancery Lane, declares that penal taxation is ephemeral, and that of the really big English properties the ownership has not changed. But Lord Arthur is aware of the price of coal and the state of the plumbing; fitfully but with an alert intelligence he conducts inquisitions in the estate office; he has followed certain financial clues through their labyrinth, and it is his conclusion that Benison is a Grace and Favour house, the patronage of which is vested in two or three powerful persons in the City. By an agreement among these, the Spendloves could be sold up tomorrow. But could he, knowing all this, control the situation any better than his father does, or than his elder brother will do, when in the fullness of time he is called home from his endless bird-watchings and other blameless idiocies in Scotland?

Lord Arthur checks himself in these musings, and turns in negligent ease to face his little flock. He has all his father's charm of manner, and although he will tire more quickly of this new family game, he is prepared to put greater finesse into it for a time.

'First it is very necessary to apologize to you about one or two things. The truth is that we are not quite straight at Benison.' And Lord Arthur meets the respectful attention of his group with a gaze the frankness of which must dispel any possible ambiguity lurking in his speech. 'In the early years of the war we had a government concern quartered on us – quite an important government concern – and after that we had a couple of schools. I didn't see much of it myself, because I was having a quiet sort of life in the desert and Tripoli and Italy. But it seems that things got pushed around a bit and stowed away and so forth; and we still don't know quite where we are.'

'Did the schoolchildren cause a lot of damage?' An elderly woman turns from fingering the long gold curtains of the music-room to ask this question.

'Oh, no – dear me, no.' Lord Arthur's glance has travelled over his hearers' heads – he is inches taller than any of them – to the long line of paintings on the north wall. They no longer correspond with the faded patches on the green silk behind them, and he sees too that Canova's frigid Aphrodite has been shoved into the corner formerly occupied by Flaxman's bust of the elder Pitt. He is assailed by the renewed conviction that he and his family are now only camping in Benison, even that they are unlawful squatters who may at any time be evicted by the police; that they may be required to pack up their improvised domesticities and quit – trundling the Aphrodite, and Pitt if he can be found, down the league-long drive on a wheelbarrow. The vision of his father doing this rises before him, and hurtling in the other direction he sees an unending line of motor-coaches, crammed with citizens feeling in their pockets for small change. When the Ministry took over in 1939, he is thinking, my father expected the whole place to be blown sky-high within a week. But it wasn't to be, and Benison is going to end not with a bang but a whimper.

Fortunately he is still talking. He hears his own voice insisting on how agreeable the schoolchildren were, revealing that some of them still write, still come back and inquire about horses, dogs, gardeners. Lord Arthur has the inventiveness of his father, into whose head will come nonsense about family ghosts or Noah's Ark. But he has too a streak of artistry. As he tells how the bigger girls played Sheridan in gowns which had for two centuries been laid away in lavender, or how the smaller girls were allowed to paint with their water-colours the *putti* that play hide and seek round the tall marble chimneypiece in Queen Caroline's Drawing-room, or how, treasured in the library, there is a sound-strip of a hundred young voices echoing in the great gallery : as Lord Arthur tells of these things he makes them golden – as golden as the light now pouring in level shafts across the park – Claude's light, the light of the great ideal landscapes, glinting on the gold-leaf that sheaths the high windows without, on the gold damask that drapes them within, on the long lines of gilt frames on the walls, on furniture here smothered and here licked with gold. The great room is full of the golden light. But soon it will be fading and everybody will go away. Already from the nearer stretches of the park comes the pulse and throb of engines, as if the pasturing *chars-à-bancs* were raising their heads and lowing – lowing to be led to some milking-parlour mightier than that erected by the sixth Marquis of Scattergood in the Chinese taste.

And presently this is answered by another sound. From a distant court of the great building – a court palatial in itself, but here serving for offices and stables – a deep-toned bell is calling the hour in long golden syllables that carry through Benison's two hundred rooms, roll across its spreading formal gardens, its ornamental waters, and its spacious park, to die finally into a just perceptible vibration in the distant streets and houses of Benison Magna, Benison Parva, Abbot's Benison, and Candleshoe.

# CHAPTER TWO

'IF that wasn't a darn queer thing!' Grant Feather slows down behind a *char-à-banc* on the Palladian Bridge. 'What makes them put in time, do you think, taking round a raggle-taggle of tourists like you and me?'

With her nose still in her guide-book, Mrs Feather absently shakes her head. 'The Temple of Ancient Virtue', she reads, 'was designed by Kent. Now, why didn't we see that? A graceful but massive structure. The Temple of Modern Virtue was constructed nearby in the form of a ruin, the contrast being allegorical in intention. It was removed by the seventh marquess, who intended to erect in its place a Temple of Progress and Perfectibility. His interests changed however and he built a mosque, now used as a cow-shed. I'd say that folks crazy enough to do things like that are crazy enough to take round tourists.'

'You agree, momma, that it was a mite crazy?'

'Well, Grant, it was courteous too. If you're good enough to be let in at all, even at half a dollar, you're good enough to be talked to. Your grandfather would have done the same, if he'd ever felt like collecting half-dollars from people wanting to see round his house at Newport.'

'Nobody would want to see round that house at Newport.'

'They might now. Your grandfather's house is almost as much a period piece as Benison.' Mrs Feather turns the page of her guide-book. 'The chapel is by Wren, and contains a fine statuary group by Roubiliac. We didn't see that either.'

Grant Feather sets his foot on the accelerator and chuckles. 'Perhaps that's another half-dollar. After all, Benison isn't just one period piece. It's several.' He stops the car. 'There's your last glimpse of it.'

They have driven for two miles through the park, and lodge-gates and the public highway are just in front of them. On their left is a broad sheet of ornamental water, part balustraded and part overhung by dark-foliaged trees. Small islands support obelisks, groups of statuary, miniature temples. Beyond, the river winds gently through a valley whose wooded slopes, artfully converging as the scene recedes, finally form the wings of a theatre in which the backcloth is Benison itself – the great house in all its incredible length and high Ionic elegance planted squarely to the view, with only the open sky behind the bold symmetry of its central mass, its spreading wings, its end pavilions.

For a moment Mrs Feather contemplates the large assertion of it in silence. Then she snaps shut the guide-book. 'I was wrong. Period piece isn't the name for it. It's a show-place.'

'Well, I guess it's that too.' Grant is amused by what he discerns as a change of mood in his mother. 'And grandfather's Newport mansion is hardly that.'

'Benison was a show-place from the start, and that's why that old man must go on showing it now. He'd prefer a more time-sanctioned ostentation – big parties of his own sort, with fifty house-maids staggering up and down those great staircases with coal-scuttles, and everything very grand and splendid. But that's no longer possible in England. And rather than have his great house degenerate into something useful – say an orphanage or a convalescent home – '

Grant Feather lets in his clutch again and shouts with laughter. He is from Harvard; he has finished his first year at Oxford; it pleases him to pretend that his mother is a cosy little woman, much lacking in sophistication. 'Rather than do that, the old boy continues to show off – but to new classes of society?'

'Just that. You see, Benison isn't really old – and those

Spendloves aren't really old either, or at least they ain't old as the biggest sort of aristocrats are. When you get true antiquity – '

Mrs Feather has again provoked an explosion of mirth in her son. 'A single thirst for modernity distinguishes the American at home, and a single passion for antiquity grips him when abroad.'

'Grant, you got that from your Oxford tutor.'

'Perhaps I did.' Grant grins. 'But it's true, all the same. "What is the oldest thing you have here?" I heard one of our countrymen fire that at the old marquess an hour ago. Or there was the woman that pointed at a portrait of Margaret Plantagenet and asked if she came of an old family. And now here's you complaining that Benison Court misses out on the owls and ivy.'

'That's not quite why I find I don't like it.' Mrs Feather settles back comfortably as the car swings into the highway. 'If it's a period-piece, it's a period-piece of the show-place period. Do you get that?'

'I get the ostentation. Benison makes its gesture half-across its tight little county.'

'That's just it. Rather a blatant gesture. Right at the end of that century – the seventeenth century – the English sense of values deteriorates. They begin putting up big empty vulgar things, and demanding admiration for their mere size and expensiveness. Mind you, Grant, I think it may have been largely our fault.'

'*Our* fault?' Grant takes his eyes from the road to glance at his mother in astonishment.

'For quitting. For crossing the Atlantic, and draining England of the folk with the old, mature sense of values. English society has been kind of raw ever since.'

'Perhaps we should come back?'

'Perhaps we should.' Mrs Feather considers it seriously. 'After all, they wouldn't put us in the pillory any more, or burn our books, or stop us going to church. You might figure it, Grant, that the practical reasons for our exile being past and done with, it's our business to pack up and come home.'

'You would advocate founding a new England on the western seaboard of this island? You would push back the savages of Lancashire and Cumberland into Yorkshire and Northumberland?' Grant pauses for a moment to peer at a sign-post. 'But you wouldn't like it, momma. The immemorial spirit of the place would take charge, and presently you would find that your new England was being run by men. The great American Matriarchy would have perished in the resettlement.'

Mrs Feather opens her guide-book again as a gesture of scorn. The Matriarchy joke always offends her. For some minutes the car travels in silence, and then she makes a discovery. 'The church at Abbot's Benison has long-and-short work.'

'Has what?'

'A stonemason's technique not found in England after the Saxon period.'

'Sure – Owl-and-Ivy. Do you know, I kind of get it mixed with Decorated and Perpendicular. Well, it's just too bad we missed Abbot's Benison.'

'Second on the left, and then left again, will take us straight back to it.' Mrs Feather is inflexible. 'There is a three-decker Jacobean pulpit.'

'That's fine. But these English hotels, remember, believe in something called the dinner-hour. If we miss – '

'And an elaborate marble monument, with curious original iron-work, is believed to be by Gerard Christmas, carver to the navy. I was reading about him only the other day.'

With a sigh of resignation Grant swings the car left. His mother's indefatigable antiquarianism at once delights and bores him. 'You know,' he says presently, 'if you lived in this country, you'd never go after all these period pieces and show-places and churches with Owl-and-Ivy work. Your bondage to them would be broken, and you could sit quietly at home, toasting your ten toes before a nice English open fire. Why not settle for a year or two and try it? Your own little experiment in the new New England.'

'Now, Grant, that's a curious thing. I've been thinking as we drove along this morning that Oxford has a great attraction for me. And last week I was shown a very nice apartment there, right opposite the gates of your college. And the society would be attractive, too. Your dear old President and his wife, and your tutor, and a heap of your own friends.'

With a quick glance Grant assures himself that this devastating idea is a product of his mother's sense of humour. 'Oxford has plenty of Owl-and-Ivy, sure enough. But would it give you scope, momma? You'd do better to buy Benison.'

'You think it's for sale?' Mrs Feather speaks with the prosaic interest of one who would have no difficulty in finding the money – and she is, as it happens, an extremely wealthy woman.

'They'd jump at a good price, and retire to Corbies and the family ghost with the bagpipes. Or you might rent the place, and bind Lord Scattergood to live in one of the lodges and continue to act as chief guide.'

'Benison isn't at all what I want. And none of the places I've looked at is *quite* right.'

Grant stares. 'You've *really* looked?'

'I went over several manor-houses in the Cotswolds last week. If your sisters follow you over here, a house will be a convenience. But those I've seen have all had something – well, subtly wrong with them.'

'Something spurious about the immemorial flavour?'

'That – and their being kind of thrust at you. I want to *find* a house. That, you know, is what a period piece is – something that you yourself rescue from oblivion, and that quite perfectly recalls its own epoch because it has been unregarded and uninterfered with ever since. . . . Look out!'

They are on a winding secondary road and Grant, driving well, is not really in danger of an accident. But he has to brake hard, and the boy who has burst out of a hedge on his near side is lucky to have got across without at least a bad fright. He is through the opposite hedge now, and in a moment he vanishes. Grant changes gear and drives on.

'Wasn't that rather a queer boy?' Mrs Feather's voice is perplexed. 'Did you notice?'

'I didn't notice much about him. Reckless little brute.'

'He had a cap.'

'Why shouldn't he?'

'I don't think that English country boys much wear them. And it had a long feather in it. And he had long stockings that looked almost like – '

Grant is aware that his mother has broken off in order to concentrate her attention upon some object, apparently in the middle distance, that lies over his shoulder. He glances in the same direction and sees nothing but a hawthorn hedge, and beyond this a beech copse in which the shadows of evening are beginning to gather. Recalling the celerity with which the less unpalatable dishes are prone to be 'off' in English hotels, he accelerates. But his mother lays a hand on his arm. 'Grant – do stop. It's Jacobean.'

He stops, and Mrs Feather at once gets out of the car. He follows and sees rising above the beeches two chimney-stacks in cut brickwork, each of them of three grouped shafts. They rise boldly above a scroll-work gable which can just be glimpsed through the tree-tops, and the evening sun catches them so that the mellow red above the foliage is like flame. Children's voices can be heard in the distance, but the evening is curiously still and the beech copse has an air of mystery. Mrs Feather is entranced and Grant is apprehensive. 'If you really want to see the church at Abbot's Benison – ' he begins.

But his mother shakes her head. Without taking her eyes from the peeping gable and its clustered chimneys, she feels in the car for her guide-book. 'If it hadn't been for that boy, we'd have gone by without noticing it. Did you ever see a place that had such an air of being hidden away?'

Grant does not audibly assent to this; he sees the looming danger of trespass, barbed wire, torn clothes, detection, embarrassment. He has been through it before. So he reaches for a map and studies it. 'Three miles to Abbot's Benison,' he presently announces. 'And two miles short of that there's a hamlet called Candleshoe.'

'Candleshoe?' Mrs Feather's delight deepens. 'Isn't that a wonderful name?'

'I don't find it all that striking, momma. And that house, if you want to know, must be Candleshoe Manor.'

Mrs Feather consults her guide-book. 'This says nothing about it. Yet I'm sure it's Jacobean. It may even be Elizabethan.'

'And good Queen Bess herself may have slept here?' Grant moves back towards the car. 'Well, if it isn't mentioned, it can't be on show. So we may as well move on.'

'But, Grant, that means we've practically discovered it.'

'Nonsense. There will be some big county history with screeds about it. But that doesn't mean that the folk who live here want inquisitive trippers poking round.'

'Perhaps nobody lives here. They say a lot of these places are deserted and going to rack and ruin. Would that be some sort of drive fifty yards down the road?' Mrs Feather sets off at a brisk pace as she speaks. 'I believe it is. And there's a lodge.'

Resigning himself to the situation, Grant steps out beside her. The road appears wholly unfrequented, and he recalls that he has seen no other vehicle since branching off on it. The boy – according to his mother, the oddly dressed boy – is the only sign of life that has appeared. And the lodge, when they come up to it, is clearly deserted; the windows are boarded up and a hole gapes in the roof. Even his mother acknowledges it to be a nondescript of no antiquarian interest; she opines that it is a nineteenth-century affair, built when some secondary approach to the house was constructed by a prosperous owner. On each side of the drive itself a masonry column of undistinguished proportions attests to a sort of perfunctory grandeur; one is topped by a meaningless stone ball and from the other an identical ball has toppled and lies half-buried in grass. Rusted hinges show that there must once have been a pair of iron gates. But these have vanished and there is open access to a cart-track – it appears little more – that presently takes a twist among the beech-trees and vanishes. The house can no longer be seen.

'We'll just look what's round that bend.' Mrs Feather is still briskly resolved. But in response to the silence that seems to be gathering round them she has unconsciously lowered her voice. A rabbit not twenty yards ahead nibbles undisturbed, and for a moment the intruders find themselves standing quite still in tingling expectation. It is a drift of primitive feeling that has worked its way upwards into their eminently civilized consciousness; were it to break in on a more substantial scale they would experience panic, and the god himself might catch and claim them as they bolted for their car. But this passes; they set off up the neglected avenue; the rabbit vanishes; Mrs Feather gives a moment's attention to the commonplace business of finding half-a-crown.

'Probably it is deserted. But there may be a caretaker,

and he will be glad enough to show us round. There will be quite enough daylight, although it is already dusky here in the trees.'

Grant says nothing. He sees only cold corned beef, watery salad, blancmange, and the crowning horror known as 'jelly' between himself and bedtime. These will be served in penitential conditions by an obtrusively promoted scullion in an empty dining-room depressingly 'laid' for breakfast.

They have reached the bend and rounded it. A few yards ahead a tree-trunk sprawls dead across the drive; it is a barrier which they must scramble over if they are to go further. Grant supposes that it must have been brought down by a storm, but when his eye travels to its base he sees that this is not so, and that it has been expertly felled to lie as it now does. He and his mother both come to a halt; as they do so there is an odd twang in the air somewhere to their left, and they are looking at the shaft of an arrow quivering in the obstacle before them.

'That's your boy with the queer cap.' Grant is at once clear-headed about this surprising occurrence. 'And it has a message.' He advances to the tree-trunk and takes hold of the arrow. It is home-made, powerful, and correctly feathered; it pierces and has carried a twist of paper. Grant tears this off and unfolds it. They are looking at a single word scrawled in pencil:

*Avaunt!*

'An inhospitable boy.' Mrs Feather frowns. 'But where would a village child come by a word like that?'

Grant laughs. 'From a five-cent story of Robin Hood and his merry men, I'd guess. And I don't suppose it's meant to be ambiguous.'

'How could it be ambiguous?' Mrs Feather turns colloquial. 'Don't it just mean *"Git"*?'

'It might mean *"Advance"*.' Grant is on ground where

his education excels his mother's. 'Spenser uses it that way in the *Faerie Queene*.'

'I never heard of village boys reading the *Faerie Queene*.'

'This mayn't be a village boy. It may be the young lord of the manor, amusing himself in a mildly alarming way at our expense. The way they said "Trespassers will be prosecuted" in Sherwood Forest long ago.'

'We'll take it to mean the other thing, and go right ahead.' Mrs Feather's resolution is mounting. She climbs over the tree and walks on.

*Twang!*

This time the arrow gives the impression of having travelled uncomfortably close to their ears. But its mark has been at a discreet distance ahead; Grant goes forward to the standing tree in which this time it has lodged, and again finds a message. He twists it open and reads:

> 'Enter these enchanted woods,
> You who dare!'

'Meredith.' It is apparent that in the way of English poetry Grant Feather knows all the answers. 'And this time I'd say it *is* ambiguous – a kind of challenge. But will it be safe to accept?' Grant looks at his mother as whimsically as he can. In fact, he is uneasy. He knows that the bow and arrow at work are not the sort with which a child plays in a suburban garden. The thing could be lethal. And the child may be cracked. He does not want this Robin Hood ballad stuff to turn into a Cock Robin nursery rhyme to his mother's personal hazard.

Mrs Feather divines that her son is feeling protective. This amuses her, but she is diplomatic. 'We can risk it. The boy has certainly gotten a powerful bow. But a challenge like that doesn't come to the mind of anyone who is going to shoot you in the back. We'll go straight ahead.'

Strictly, this is not a feasible programme, for the drive,

such as it is, pursues a winding course. Perhaps it was originally constructed in this way in order to give a false impression of distance; it is twisting about in the beech wood so as to make the most of it.

They move forward. No more arrows are fired. Mrs Feather has taken the second message from her son, and now she glances at it. 'Grant – can you remember any more of this poem?'

'Quite a lot.' He is aware that his voice has gone self-conscious in what they feel as a deepening circumambient silence. But he firmly begins to quote :

> 'Enter these enchanted woods,
> You who dare.
> Nothing harms beneath the leaves
> More than waves a swimmer cleaves.
> Toss your heart up with the lark,
> Foot at peace with mouse and worm,
> Fair you fare.'

Mrs Feather listens attentively as she walks. 'It's an odd sort of poetry to appeal to a boy.'

'Didn't you say he was an odd sort of boy?' And Grant continues to recite :

> 'Only at a dread of dark
> Quaver, and they quit their form :
> Thousand eyeballs under hoods
> Have you by the hair.
> Enter these enchanted woods,
> You who dare.'

'I see.' Mrs Feather is appreciative. 'The whole poem is a kind of challenge. Perhaps Candleshoe Manor will be that too.' She pauses, as if aware that in this remark there is a flavour of vagueness alien to her normal personality. 'How very still the place is! One can imagine there is never a sound in this wood from dawn to dusk.'

'But plenty from dusk to dawn?' And Grant, who

wants to show off his stock of poetry, begins to quote again :

> 'Sudden will a pallor pant
> Chill at screeches miscreant ;
> Owls or spectres, thick they flee ;
> Nightmare upon horror broods ;
> Hooded laughter, monkish glee,
>     Gaps the vital air.
>   Enter these enchanted woods,
>       You . . .'

Grant breaks off abruptly. The notable silence into which he is declaiming has been as notably broken. Somewhere quite close at hand a bell is tolling – a small, cracked bell.

# CHAPTER THREE

THE bell is cracked and insignificant. But unlike the majestic bell at Benison its tintinnabulation is unmistakably a call to some religious observance. It is at once authoritative and domestic – first cousin to a dinner-bell and yet indubitably of the Church. It speaks of a parson tugging at a rope with one hand while stuffing away his pipe and reaching for his surplice with the other. Mrs Feather, whose historical imagination has been so inadequately gratified in the course of the afternoon, suddenly feels that she has heard the very heart-beat of England. Her eyes fill with tears, and she has to cope with these before taking a glance at her son. Is he at all impressed? At Oxford he is exposed to quite a lot of bell-ringing, and if he returns there in thirty years time the sounds will move him unspeakably. But this he may feel to be only an ugly little clamour. Mrs Feather cannot tell. She rounds another bend, and finds a miniature church or chapel before her. Like the lodge it is in disrepair, with windows for the most part boarded up and a hole in the roof. Nevertheless something is going on in it. In a little belfry the small jangling bell is just ceasing to swing.

'It seems to be joined on.' Grant is pointing vaguely ahead. A tall hedge – it may be either box or yew – interposes between them and the main building beyond, and in the fading light the character and topography of the place are alike hard to determine. But on the far side of the chapel some sort of covered way may be descried, and it is to this that he is pointing.

'Almshouses!' Light comes to Mrs Feather. 'One of those immemorial charities. And the poor old almoners – isn't that the word . . . ?'

'It certainly is not. Inmates – or beadsmen.'

'The poor old beadsmen have to attend chapel twice a day and pray for the soul of the founder.'

'Would they be allowed to do that in an Anglican church?' Grant is interested. 'I mean, if it had been laid down when the charity started in Catholic times?'

'We can go in and find out. The old people must be there now.'

'Say – we can't do that!' Grant is horrified. 'It's no business of ours.'

'Public and corporate worship is anybody's business.' As Mrs Feather delivers herself of this pious if convenient sentiment she is already on the march again. 'I expect there are old women too. And no doubt strangers may attend and contribute. There will be a box. Now, what did I do with that half-crown?'

Recollection comes to Grant. 'It can't be almshouses. The map says – '

He is too late. Mrs Feather, whom he still follows obediently, has reached the little chapel, found an open door, and marched in. Some sort of service is indubitably going forward. Grant is aware that his mother, with unusual precipitancy, has sat down, and that he himself is perched beside her on a hard bench of quite inadequate breadth. He is aware too of a high quavering voice speaking of the absolution and remission of sins. He knows that he is attending Evening Prayer according to the form of the Church of England. He takes a deep breath and looks about him for the almsfolk of his mother's imagining, although with small hope of finding them. And of course he is right. It is a private chapel. He has never been in such a place before. But he recognizes it in an instant.

At Benison the chapel is by Wren and there is a statuary group by Roubiliac. This is different. It is like the smallest and most unassuming parish church in a Decorated style – 'Decorated' only in the technical sense, since the actual effect is bare enough. There is a single monument – and at

a first glance it appears to be of the order described in Mrs
Feather's guide-books as 'rude'. Grant studies it; he has a
hunch that it is the least embarrassing thing available for
study. A gentleman with flowing locks and a completely
composed demeanour is raising himself from a stony
ocean and grasping the prows of a vessel which appears
to be in the act of foundering. Upon this watery scene two
younger gentlemen standing on either hand are about to
lower a pair of marble curtains. Crowning this is a coat of
arms, decorated in faded gold and colour – and this
Grant, although without much learning in such matters,
feels to be obscurely familiar.

And now he lets his glance stray further afield. Along
one wall the chapel contains two benches such as one
might find in a village school, and it is on one of these
that he and his mother are sitting. The rest of the furnish-
ing consists of the altar, a lectern, and three mouldering
upright chairs upholstered in ragged leather. Before each
chair is an ancient and crumpled hassock upon which
either long practice or an abnormally good sense of
balance might make it possible to kneel. Only one of the
chairs is occupied – by a diminutive lady of great age.
Dressed in black silks of an answering antiquity, and with
a black lace cap set upon snow-white hair, she is deliver-
ing herself of responses in what Grant supposes to be a
provincial accent. Mrs Feather, who has been exposed to
intermittent contact with the English since childhood,
knows that it belongs not to any specific region but to the
past – to a past, she further guesses, quite surprisingly
remote. The officiating clergyman, too, suggests an earlier
time – but this less by his voice than by his attire.
Memories of some illustrated edition of Jane Austen float
through her head; as she listens to the Collect for Aid
against all Perils she finds herself surprised that the person
offering this petition wears his own hair – or a wispy remnant of that – rather than a powdered wig. She perceives

that her sense of time is becoming confused, and supposes it the effect of some delayed shock from the archery display to which she has lately been subjected.

The service is over. The little old lady rises, speaks briefly to the clergyman in inaudible tones, turns, and moves from the chapel, supporting herself on a silver-mounted ebony stick. As she passes the Feathers she bows. The weight of years has already so bent her figure that the effect is alarming. Moreover the gesture is unaccompanied by any play of feature, and without pausing the old lady walks on and disappears. The clergyman vanishes somewhere at the back.

Mrs Feather finds that she is still clutching her half-crown. She looks about her, not quite prepared to abandon the obscure hope of paying her way. 'There may be a box saying "General Expenses",' she suggests. 'Or "For the Fabric". There so often is.'

'Would you keep such a thing in your bathroom?'

'In my bathroom, Grant?' Rather feebly, Mrs Feather affects bewilderment.

'Sure. This chapel is just as private to the old lady as your bathroom is to you. Different kinds of cleanliness are in question, no doubt, in one and the other. But the idea of privacy attaches to each.' Grant makes this speech with some severity. His hopes of anything resembling a satisfactory dinner are now remote.

'Well, Grant, it did *look* like almshouses – '

'Nonsense, momma. It's just that you will keep walking on, and opening doors, until you're stopped.'

'Grant, I was opening doors in this country, and having them opened for me, I'd like to add, before you – '

'Good evening.'

The Feathers, caught in a moment of some indignity, turn round. For a second they suppose themselves to be addressed by a venerable upper servant. They then see that it is the clergyman. He has abandoned his outmoded sacerdotal habiliments for equally outmoded garments inescapably suggestive of a superannuated butler. He is however a gentleman – a very old gentleman – and he is himself now engaged in a process of social appraisal through steel-rimmed spectacles balanced precariously on the end of his nose.

'And what a beautiful day it has been. It is pleasant to think of visitors touring the country in such ideal weather. No doubt you have been to Abbot's Benison, and have come on upon hearing that we too have a fine Christmas.'

'A fine Christmas?' Mrs Feather is only momentarily at a loss. 'But yes, indeed! And is that your Christmas?' She advances upon the monument which Grant has already studied. 'I know some of his work in Buckinghamshire. That's the county one of my ancestors left in 1620.'

Whether or not he makes anything of this august date, the clergyman smiles benignly. 'You may be thinking in particular of the Clarke monument at Hitcham. But there, my dear madam, caution is necessary – caution is undoubtedly necessary. The affinity with our own monument is pronounced – you have only to glance at those figures holding the curtains to acknowledge it. But the authenticity is less well attested. We, as you may know, have the actual accounts, with a discharge in Christmas's own hand.'

If Grant were not a well-bred young man he would audibly groan. Local antiquarianism dispensed by a clerical dotard amid deepening shades of evening makes a close to the day even more depressing than corned beef and blancmange. But Mrs Feather is now in her element. 'It is a monument', she is asking, 'to a former lord of the manor?'

'Certainly – most certainly.' The ancient clergyman takes off his glasses, breathes on them from lungs still professionally robust, polishes them, and returns them to his nose upside-down. 'Admiral Candleshoe. We lost him, I am sorry to say, on the Islands Voyage. That would be – let me see – in 1597. It was a bad business – a very bad business. To be quite frank with you, we were displeased with the conduct of the Earl of Essex.'

'You were displeased with the conduct of the Earl of Essex – *Elizabeth's* Essex?' Mrs Feather is uncertain how to take this.

'Yes, indeed. But they needn't have chopped his head off four years later, all the same. By the way, my name is Armigel – Rupert Armigel.' The ancient clergyman has produced a snuff-box and is tapping it. Grant sees that because he himself carries no snuff-box there is going to be a hitch in some ritual of introduction that the old gentleman is proposing. This embarrasses him acutely; he blushes; and his mother has to come to his rescue in this matter of names.

'My name is Feather – Alice Feather – and this is my son Grant. Do you live here, Mr Armigel?'

'Assuredly – most assuredly.' The ancient clergyman pauses while Grant, who has been obliged to take a pinch of snuff, gives a sequence of sneezes that ring out startlingly in the bare chapel. 'Rupert Armigel, madam – domestic chaplain to Miss Candleshoe.'

Mrs Feather gives a cry of delight – presumably at discovering that a Candleshoe still lives at Candleshoe. Grant's embarrassment returns, and he edges away towards Gerard Christmas's monument. The foundering admiral, he realizes, bears an unmistakable family likeness to the old lady who, a few minutes before, has been worshipping here. But there is something else – some further likeness – that eludes, puzzles him.

'You judge it appropriate?' Mr Armigel is at his elbow, and now all three are confronting Admiral Candleshoe's memorial.

'It's very handsome.' Grant hopes that he has hit on the right epithet.

'I agree with you. Both as an artist, which was my first profession, and as a very old friend and – um – adherent of the Candleshoe family, I am entirely pleased with it. Moreover Miss Candleshoe herself, I am glad to say, considers that Christmas has done a very good piece of work. She considers that the thing will serve very well.'

Grant, not without satisfaction, sees something like alarm momentarily visit his mother's features. 'Has Christmas done anything else here?' he asks.

'Decidedly – most decidedly. You will see a work of considerable interest in the house itself. And that reminds me that I have been remiss – most remiss. Miss Candleshoe has desired me to invite you to take a glass of wine. I hope there *is* some wine. And perhaps we had better wait on her now.'

The Feathers make modest protestations, but Grant knows that his mother is jubilant. Once more he takes refuge in the monument – this time peering at an inscription low down on the right. The light is bad; he fails to decipher it; and Mr Armigel comes to his rescue.

'An addition, Mr Feather. A copy of modern verses which, although not inappropriate to their subject, strike, to my mind, a jarring note. Modern poetry is out of place, surely, in connexion with the Islands Voyage.'

Grant has knelt down and can now read the lettering. It is incised in an ancient character and still faintly gilt. For the second time that evening he gives himself to declaiming English verse.

> 'Aye me! whilst thee the shores and sounding seas
> Wash far away, where'er thy bones are buried;
> Whether beyond the stormy Hebrides,
> Where thou perhaps under the whelming tide ...'

Grant breaks off. 'Say! But that's Milton. I thought you said – '

Mr Armigel nods placidly. 'Quite so – precisely so. An

elegy called "Lycidas", Mr Feather. Beautiful in itself. But modern poetry is not suitable on Admiral Candleshoe's monument.'

*Enter these enchanted woods, You who dare.* ... It comes home to Grant with marked force that about Candleshoe Manor there is something a little out of the way. Perhaps the ether wobbles. Conceivably there is a kink in space. Time – at least within the consciousnesses of the residents – is far from behaving as it should. Grant gets rather hastily to his feet. Mr Armigel may be mad. Miss Candleshoe's wine may be a magic potion calculated to turn respectable pilgrims from Massachusetts into Sleeping Beauties or Rip van Winkles.

'Haven't I seen that coat of arms before?' Mrs Feather uninterested in Milton, is pointing to the upper part of the monument.

Grant follows her gesture. He remembers that he, too, has had the same impression. And suddenly he can account for it. 'The flag, momma – the Spendlove standard, flying above Benison.' He turns to Mr Armigel. 'Are the Candleshoes connected with the Spendloves, sir?'

Mr Armigel finds this amusing. He contrives the odd feat of laughing and taking snuff simultaneously. 'My dear Mr Feather, your conjecture is at once correct and preposterous.'

'I don't get that.' Grant is now sure that the old gentleman is crazy.

'Correct but upside-down, topsy-turvy, the wrong way round. The Spendloves are connected with the Candleshoes.'

Grant sees the difference. He glances again at Admiral Candleshoe and experiences a shock of discovery. Here is the other similarity that has worried him. The expiring sailor is not only like the present Miss Candleshoe of Candleshoe Manor; he is the split image of Lord Scattergood of Benison Court.

'The Spendloves are Candleshoes – but of a very junior line.' Mr Armigel, pleased to find Mrs Feather evidently entranced, appears about to embark upon genealogical disquisition. But he checks himself. 'Miss Candleshoe is waiting to receive you. She is most interested in your visit, and it will be a kindness if you will make a short call. Let me lead the way to the house.'

The Feathers, with polite murmurs, prepare to follow Mr Armigel. All three turn towards the door of the chapel, and all three pause. Framed in it, as if to bar their way, stands a boy. He is dressed in what may be Tudor costume. And he carries a bow.

# CHAPTER FOUR

ABRUPTLY the boy vanishes. Together with accurate archery, it seems to be his main accomplishment. For a moment the effect has been as of some ancient portrait; now the arched doorway of the chapel is like an empty frame, and behind it is only mild evening sky. Grant Feather frowns for a moment into this immensity, and then takes a glance back at Admiral Candleshoe. That distressed mariner has all the timelessness and immobility which the best authorities pronounce to be desirable in sculpture. He does not propose really to drown, nor on the other hand has he any genuine mind to be rescued. It is conceivable that when the chapel is void of spectators the attendant effigies will lower their marble curtains on the scene and go off duty for the night. But this fancy can be entertained only in defiance of the most powerful suggestion to the contrary. These supporting figures are frozen into the same permanence as the Admiral between them. In the first days of their existence, while Gerard Christmas was still tidying up his chisels and superintending the gilding, they must already have had the appearance of centennial vigil. Infants christened beneath their impassive gaze have come rejoicing to the command of bow and arrow and angling-rod and fowling-piece – and have returned to their presence in the end, while some predecessor of Mr Armigel's has addressed himself to the burial service.

From somewhere outside comes a sudden hubbub of young voices; it recedes, as if a bevy of children are racing and tumbling into the distance. Mr Armigel occupies himself with a bunch of keys; Mrs Feather takes the opportunity of slipping her half-crown unobstrusively back into her bag; Grant finds small comfort in this, for he suspects his mother of nursing an atrocious purpose. The coin may not be produced again at Candleshoe. But what about its near companion, Mrs Feather's cheque-book? The Spendloves at Benison are lords. But Mrs Feather's forebears for several generations have been princes – merchant-princes – and she has inherited an instinct for brisk and open commerce. Had the impulse moved her, she might have offered Lord Scattergood in his own octagon room a round figure for everything within sight. She would be capable of doing the same thing – Grant reflects with a fine imaginative flight – while being shown the Crown Jewels in the Tower of London. And she believes that she has *discovered* Candleshoe. Horridly pat, like an actor taking a heavily-signalled cue in some banal play, the place had peeped out from behind its beech-trees in the very instant that the good lady was discoursing on the satisfaction of rescuing a period piece from oblivion.

Grant does not at all object to his mother's buying a derelict English manor-house. What he has glimpsed of Candleshoe pleases him, and he knows that his sisters would adore it. But Oxford, although he is doubtless to derive large benefits from his residence there in the end, has rather muddled him for the time, and he has a morbid fear that his mother is going to do something crude. How is he to circumvent this? There comes to him the inspiration that he must be crude himself – so crude that his mother will at once be all reaction. So he turns to Mr Armigel. 'Say,' he offers conversationally, 'what sort of sanitation do you have here?'

They are walking down a short covered way of no great antiquity, and the house is in flank before them. Mrs Feather nearly drops her bag – half-crown, cheque-book, and all. She remembers that it was very hot in the gardens at Benison, and wonders anxiously if Grant has suffered a sun-stroke. Mr Armigel however appears to take the inquiry entirely in good part.

'Now, that is an interesting question – a very interesting question, indeed. Only, I think you use rather a grand word, if I may say so, for anything of the sort at Candleshoe. We never have had anything that you could quite term that.'

'Is that so, sir?'

'In fact, all that I can recall at the moment, are two or three quite small and nasty affairs.'

'I see.'

'And, of course, that sort of thing has fallen more and more out of favour in England. We have lost the taste for it. In your country, I understand, the posture of affairs is somewhat different. The thing keeps on cropping up.'

'Well, yes, sir.' Grant is rather at a loss. 'In fact we just aren't happy without it.'

'Deplorable!' Mr Armigel shakes his venerable head, and for the first time speaks with some severity. 'But I should be happy to tell you our own experiences, if your interest runs that way. They are, I fear, malodorous. And underground.'

At this Mrs Feather stops in her tracks. 'It just occurs to me', she says, 'to inquire what you suppose my son to be talking about?'

Mr Armigel turns to her courteously. 'Assassination, madam. The topic is an interesting if repulsive one. And as it is commonly applied in England only to homicide of some political or large public significance, I have remarked that it is not quite an appropriate word in a quiet place like this. But we have had our bloodstained pages, I am bound to admit.'

Grant wonders whether Mr Armigel is really a little deaf. Meanwhile they have turned aside into a ruined garden, perhaps that they may approach the house by way of its main façade. The garden is like the faded and shrunken ghost of something at Hatfield or Longford – intricately formal within a great rectangular hedge grown wild and ragged, and with all its ordered elaboration of arabesques and knots overgrown and only in part distinguishable, like a schoolchild's geometrical drawing largely obliterated by the sweep of an indiarubber. At the far end is a small pool covered with duckweed, and in the middle of this an eroded Nereid patiently clasps a lichened shell from which water has ceased to issue a long time ago. Grant recalls the gardens at Benison and their great *jet d'eau*. Presently, he thinks, time's impatient indiarubber will reach that too.

Mr Armigel discourses on certain passages of violence in the history of Candleshoe. From generation to generation the place itself has slumbered, and its owners with it. But the chronicle shows an intermittent streak of wildness among its younger sons. It is two or three of these who have, upon certain unedifying occasions, streaked the page with blood. Others have taken their waywardness to sundry remote corners of the globe, and among these – Mr Armigel intimates – an equal rashness has produced rather more that is laudable.

Mrs Feather inquires about the present heir. Grant compresses his lips, reading into this a clear proof of his mother's intention. Mr Armigel replies that the air is generally accounted wholesome, and the exposure of the mansion particularly well adapted to making the best of the winter sunshine. Grant decides that this is a cunning old man. He even suspects that there may be some plan to put Candleshoe on the market, and that any persons of evident substance straying within its policies are liable to be conducted to the owner and entertained with an eye to possible business. This however scarcely allays his anxieties about his mother's conduct. Her mind may be moving in the same way. And if they are both wrong, some humiliating situation may ensue.

But now the house is squarely before them. It is undoubtedly a gem. The plainness of the front is relieved by a central and two flanking bays, and the fine proportions of the whole are accented by the weathered stone with which the mellow brick is bonded at the major perpendiculars. There is a terrace with a crumbling arcade and a flight of steps leading down into the gardens; above the main entrance is a great dim sundial with its gnomon gone, like a battered pugilist; crowning the whole is a lettered balustrade carrying some pious Latin inscription the whole length of the building. They climb the steps, finding the broken treads only uncertainly amid weeds and moss; the main doorway is narrow, and its sides are polished by the friction of centuries of broad shoulders and hurrying elbows; on their left is a buttery hatch and on their right a high carved screen with a little staircase leading to a gallery. They pass through an opening in this screen hung with a curtain so ancient that it seems woven of dust, and find themselves in the great hall of Candleshoe Manor.

The greatness is relative. Lord Scattergood's octagon room could digest the place without noticing. But it remains a big hall, with a dais and a lofty bay window at the far end, a fireplace with a massive dog-grate, and a ceiling of elaborately moulded plaster. On the oak-panelled walls a variety of pictures – portraits and mythological scenes that have alike retreated behind a brown haze of varnish – jostle with boars' heads, foxes' masks, pikes, shields, and muskets.

There is a great deal of stuff lying about. This – Grant sees at once – makes the real point of contrast with the octagon room. That room – although very conceivably whole bevies of Spendloves smoke their pipes in it after business hours – has taken on the air of a museum; there is a great deal of stuff there too; but it is ranged and ordered, so that on each object one expects to see a little label. Here, if you are not careful, you will trip over things or bump your head. There is a lot of armour tumbled about in one corner, as if a knight in haste to get into the lists has been rummaging for a hauberk with a good snug fit. Near this a tall armoire stands open. It has been adapted – perhaps two hundred years ago – to the purposes of a wardrobe, and it contains an odd jumble of doublets and riding-cloaks and breeches, mud-bespattered and antique of cut. On the dais is a long refectory table. One end of this, extending into the bay window, catches the last warmth of the day and is laid with some elaboration for two, with silver plates and tankards, and apples in a great silver-gilt bowl. Then comes a salt-cellar – an immemorial affair of silver and horn – and below this several further places have been laid, with horn spoons and pewter mugs and great platters of polished wood.

So Miss Candleshoe is crazy. Grant Feather feels a sense of relief at being able at length to 'place' this whole queer set-up. And relief makes him charitable. 'Crazy' is perhaps an unimaginative way of putting it. Conceivably Miss Candleshoe is the last of the major English eccentrics, about whom Dr Edith Sitwell wrote so engaging a book. Grant is for some reason sure that his mother will behave impeccably in the presence of a positive strangeness of this sort. He therefore cheers up, and is about to make some polite remark when a voice speaks – or hisses – behind him.

'Strangers – beware!'

Grant looks over his shoulder. An animal of alarming proportions – he takes it to be a wolf-hound – has come through the carved oak screen behind him and is regarding him with disfavour. For a moment it seems necessary to return to the magical hypothesis and suppose Miss Candleshoe to be the mistress of some species of Circean enchantment. The dog however offers no further observation, and it occurs to Grant to look upwards. The screen, as he has noticed, supports a small minstrels' gallery. This is now shrouded in gloom, but just perceptible in it are

45

several pairs of bright eyes. Grant raises an arm and waves to them, since this strikes him as the amiable thing to do. They vanish. The archer, it appears, commands auxiliary forces as nimble as himself.

Mr Armigel and Mrs Feather have walked on. Their goal appears to be some farther room beyond the hall, and Grant remembers that in an Elizabethan mansion the private apartments lie in that direction. The other side of the house is for the servants, and at each end a staircase will rise through the several storeys of the edifice to the long gallery which must run its full length at the top. Grant sees his sisters wanting to hold a dance in the long gallery, and being told that under the weight of such a proceeding the floor will certainly collapse and bring the greater part of the house down with it. They will demand that architects and builders be brought in. And presently the whole county – which is what, if you are grand enough, you must call your neighbours – will be laughing at the antics of the folk that have bought out the Candleshoes. Grant relapses into gloom. In this mood he follows his mother into Miss Candleshoe's drawing-room.

Miss Candleshoe may worship in eighteenth-century style, dine in a fashion notably feudal, and suffer armour to lie about as other untidy people do ulsters and gumboots and shooting sticks. But when she withdraws from these occasions it is into a privacy that is wholly Victorian. There is a tartan carpet which Grant finds baffling, but which Mrs Feather is able to date as shortly after 1868, the year in which was published an illustrated edition of *Leaves from the Journal of our Life in the Highlands*. There is a further testimony to the same influence in an engraving after Landseer, depicting Prince Albert in the pose of a successful lion-hunter, standing beside a shot stag. An upholstered sofa, even after nearly a century of use, is like a fat boy in imminent danger of bursting all his buttons. On sundry small round tables, under inverted glass bowls, repose heaps of strawberries ingeniously manufactured from felt and peaches blushing in scarcely faded plush. Viewed in this setting Miss Candleshoe, who now rises to greet her guests, swims at last into something like plausible chronological focus. She is simply a very old lady who carries her own period about with her. Perhaps, like her chaplain, she drops in, as it were, on other periods from time to time. But that is a privilege of the very old.

'How do you do?' Miss Candleshoe advances with the aid of her ebony stick. She has always been what her generation would have called *petite*, and now she is so stooped – virtually, Grant thinks, into the form of an inverted capital L – as to bear the appearance of something indecisively quadrupedal moving about near the floor. But out of this posture Miss Candleshoe manages to extract more of dignity than pathos. And although doubtless a dotty old thing, she contrives an upward glance of considerable penetration from a pair of very clear black eyes which frame a powerfully hooked nose. Admiral Candleshoe, Grant remembers, has the same nose. Perhaps, before his translation into Gerard Christmas's stony immortality, he had the same eyes too.

'How do you do? Mr Armigel and I were gratified that you joined us at service. And you now add the further kindness of a call.' Miss Candleshoe raises a hand above her head and shakes hands with Mrs Feather. 'It is particularly good of your grandson to come. Youth has many calls.'

'Grant feels, as I do, that it is a privilege to see Candleshoe.' Mrs Feather declines to find malice in her hostess's disposition to treat her as a contemporary. 'It is just such a house as I have dreamed of for a long, long time.'

Grant Feather grinds his teeth. But neither Miss Candleshoe nor Mr Armigel notice this, since they are engaged in accommodating the visitors with tightly upholstered chairs, massively rich plum-cake, and glasses of wine. Grant suspects that this last may be distilled from cowslips; he sips it and discovers it to be Madeira of a sort superior to that commonly available to junior members of the University of Oxford. Perhaps Madeira lasts for ever, and this was laid down in the eighteenth century. It may have been about then that the cake was baked.

'You must not be anxious about the horses.' Miss Candleshoe herself takes a large slice of plum-cake. This however proves to be for the wolf-hound, who has taken up a posture rather like that of the Prince Consort in the engraving above him. 'My people will see to your carriage, and look after the animals very well.'

Mrs Feather is delighted. 'That is very kind of you. As a matter of fact – '

'Although naturally, since the death of my brother Sir James, we have a trifle retrenched in the stables. I do not myself hunt. Nor does Mr Armigel care to do so, although it is a customary and very proper diversion for the clergy. Of cock-fighting I do not approve. Nor should a clergyman – I speak, of course, of the Established Church – attend bouts of fisticuffs.'

'In this, fortunately, we are of one mind.' Mr Armigel appears to find nothing out-of-the-way in the sequence of his patroness's thoughts. 'But I regret the desuetude of the bowling-green.'

'The gardeners must see to it.' Miss Candleshoe pauses and sips Madeira. 'If there *are* any gardeners, that is to say. Since my brother Sir James died several years ago we have been obliged a little to cut down on one side and another. But the topiary, at least, is in tolerable order. The children, I am told, see to that.'

Here is something about which Grant wants to know. 'Then you do have kids living here?' he asks.

'At the moment, only a solitary goat.' Mr Armigel

seems to offer this reply in perfectly good faith. 'But the poultry are very flourishing, I am glad to say.'

'Only this morning, indeed, we had boiled eggs for breakfast.' Miss Candleshoe makes this announcement with an innocent triumph somewhat at odds with her *grande dame* manner. 'If we had a cow we might have some butter – in which event *scrambled* eggs would become a distinct possibility. Unfortunately the death of my brother Sir James made it necessary to dispose of the home farm.'

'Living in this wonderful old house has its inconveniences for you?' Mrs Feather is all sympathy.

Miss Candleshoe may be observed as giving her visitor a very penetrating glance indeed. 'The times are indubitably adverse to the landed interest. My brother Sir James tells me – has told me, I ought to say – that much of the blame must be attributed to Mr Gladstone. I am surprised. I had understood Mr Gladstone to indulge a taste for arboriculture, a pursuit very proper in a country gentleman of the soundest principles. But it appears that his activities were rather those of a woodcutter – or what you, doubtless, would term a lumberjack. Little good will come of a man who murders trees.'

'I just adore trees.' Mrs Feather is unblushing. 'But perhaps there is some smaller and more convenient house on the estate, which might, with a little capital – '

Grant, with great presence of mind, gives a vicious but unobstrusive kick at the wolf-hound's behind. The brute leaps up, contrives a deft outflanking movement, and bites Grant firmly in the corresponding part of his own person. There is a good deal of confusion. But this it would be tedious to retail. We may take advantage of the interlude for a necessary retrospective glance over some centuries of English history. We shall then be in a position to meet Jay Ray, the boy with the bow, and the hero – after a fashion – of this story.

# CHAPTER FIVE

IT cannot be maintained that Queen Elizabeth the First slept at Candleshoe Manor. The present house, replacing one of unknown appearance and uncertain antiquity, was completed only in the year of her death. But her successor, the canny James of Scotland, on his journey south condescended to pause there for a bever or light refection. This illustrious and somewhat expensive occasion was without consequences of any kind; neither royal favour nor royal disfavour ever visited Candleshoe again; as the house settled firmly upon its foundations it settled too into the comfortable security of near-oblivion.

Three centuries had been required for the Candleshoes to reach the modest magnificence which the place represented. When in the year 1367 a younger son was born to the Black Prince, it is upon record that the vessel bearing the news from Bordeaux belonged to one Roger Candleshoe, a vintner of Cheapside – 'long-time well-reputed', we are told, as an importer of the red wines of the Gironde. Forty-three years later, when the royal infant thus heralded met the fate of a deposed king at Pontefract, Roger's son William had added to the family trade a profitable importing of the wines of Spain – described by an expert Customs official, Geoffrey Chaucer, as of considerably greater 'fumosity' than their northern neighbours. It was when one of William Candleshoe's novelties known as sherris sack was acclaimed by a leading connoisseur of the day that the modest Candleshoe fortunes became secure. Candleshoe Manor, in fact, would never have been built had not an early fifteenth-century Candleshoe enjoyed the lavish custom and earned the generous approbation of Sir John Falstaff.

It would appear to have been not long after the death

of the good Sir John that the family acquired those lands upon which, as we may presume, they had originally laboured for others. By the close of the sixteenth century their connexion with the wine-trade had disappeared. When in the year 1600 Robert Candleshoe decided to demolish what must have been for many generations his family's home and erect in its place a more commodious mansion in the refined taste of the time, it was to his resources as landowner that he looked to defray the cost. His calculations may not have been unsound in themselves, although it is notable that he was a younger son, entered upon the inheritance only as a consequence of the death by drowning of his brother the Admiral, and committing himself to the ambitious project within three years of that melancholy circumstance. But if not a rash builder, he was certainly an injudiciously fond father; and the over-lavish provision which he endeavoured to make for most of his twelve children in fact crippled the estate to an extent from which it was never to recover.

Of these children the youngest was called Rupert; and he alone got nothing at all, except a little Latin and much fustigation from a resident tutor grown grey in the purveying of these amenities to elder brothers. Nobody disliked Rupert, or indeed much noticed him; and when at fifteen he was eventually packed off to apprenticeship in the city, the action was motivated only by the plain fact that there was nothing else to do with him. As it happened, young Rupert disliked his master, a highly respectable goldsmith with a technique of fustigation much in advance of the ageing tutor's; and the boy with great good sense almost immediately ran away. Being reduced in consequence to a somewhat hungry tramping of the London streets, he recalled the origins of his family's former prosperity in malmsey and sack, and betaking himself to the appropriate quarter of the town he accepted employment without articles in the establishment of a wine-merchant carrying on a large trade with the citizen classes. Being here set to the business of improving his firm's commodities by the judicious admixture of resins, molasses, red clay, salt-petre, and rainwater, he laboured so successfully at these mysteries as to become a person of much consideration in the city, and eventually its Lord Mayor. Rupert's son William inherited both the wealth and the address of his father. Marrying a certain Lady Elizabeth Spendlove, and acquiring her considerable fortune for his children on condition of taking her name, he further improved matters by disposing of her person to his sovereign, with the result that Charles the Second, shortly before his death, created the Lord Mayor's son first Baron Spendlove. After this the family, in the vulgar phrase, never looked back. Within a century of this well-deserved ennoblement, a certain Rupert Spendlove, son of that William, first Earl of Benison who built Benison Court, was created the first Marquess of Scattergood. A wit and a philosopher, the patron of Gay, and the friend of Bolingbroke and Swift, the first Marquess derived urbane amusement from his relationship with a neighbouring squire, and the Mr and Mrs Candleshoe of the time were occasionally invited even to the very grandest Benison occasions. Throughout the later eighteenth and earlier nineteenth centuries, indeed, young Candleshoes in quest of either a clerical or a military career would be given an amiable upward kick from Benison. One of them, a lad of parts, eventually became a bishop. In those days a marquess could do a great deal.

All this – or nearly all this – the Reverend Mr Armigel, domestic chaplain to Miss Candleshoe of Candleshoe Manor, has now expounded (by way of supplement to dabs of iodine, strips of adhesive plaster, and commiserating chuckles) to Grant Feather. Mrs Feather has meanwhile received a sufficient modicum of the same historical intelligence from her hostess to be more enchanted than ever. She takes a just pride in her ability to understand the complexity of the social system involved. The Candleshoes are confessedly bankrupt, and they are intermittently patronized by the Spendloves, whose bankruptcy is only to be conjectured, and who belong to a rank of society (Mrs Feather is quite clear about this) only just below the dukes and duchesses. But in the high dry light of genealogical science the Candleshoes, although far from shining with the first brilliance, shine distinguishably brighter than the Spendloves. An inconsiderable Candleshoe became a Spendlove, and Spendloves subsequently acquired sundry territorial tags, as of Benison and Scattergood. Is the present Miss Candleshoe in a sense the head of the family to which the present Lord Scattergood belongs? Mrs Feather confesses to herself that on a question so recondite as this she is frankly at sea. But she is at least aware of the question, and there is merit in that. She is aware too of a possible high significance attaching to the fact that the present proprietor of Candleshoe is an unmarried lady. To obtain further information here, however, requires some delicacy of approach. She waits until her hostess, with a solicitude incumbent upon the owner of the peccant hound, makes further reference to the absent Grant. She then embarks upon some general observation about her son.

'Grant won't at all mind that mite of attention from your dog – certainly not from a fine dog like that. Grant can take some hard knocks without complaining. He's an open-air boy, although fond of his books as well. Grant has a fancy to be a writer. And I'm prepared to back him in that. Only I do wish I had another son to take control of some of the family concerns.'

'*Some* of the family concerns?' Miss Candleshoe is gratifyingly interrogative.

'Not perhaps the railroad interests. Nor even the oil.

But I did have a fancy he might spend a year or two looking after the ranches. The Feathers have always enjoyed raising cattle. They pack more of it than most other folk, but they've always preferred to deal with it when still on the hoof. Coming myself from people who have never gone outside steel, I find that attractive. When my husband was alive, we used to spend weeks in the saddle, getting round one place or another.'

Miss Candleshoe's glance goes to the decanter. She is conceivably reflecting that her visitor is worth another glass. But she contents herself with regretting her own lack of acquaintance with the American colonies.

Mrs Feather accepts this as an entirely gracious observation. 'And until this present generation there always have been Feathers to take over. And that's a great thing. Property – landed property, say – must always mean less when there isn't an heir.'

Miss Candleshoe remarks that commonly there is an heir somewhere. When an heir seems to be lacking in England, one generally turns up from across the Atlantic. Persons of rustic or menial conditions have been known so to turn up – she believes from what Mrs Feather would call the prairies – and make successful claims on earldoms and baronies. But such episodes, which are on the whole to be deprecated, rarely occur among the landed gentry.

It is clear to Mrs Feather that Miss Candleshoe takes a poor view of the nobility. Mrs Feather makes a note to suppress her own devious connexion with an Irish peerage – a circumstance upon which she has at times found it advantageous to touch – and to bring in the Buckinghamshire squires when opportunity offers. Meanwhile she sets out upon a further exploratory movement. 'I do know, of course, how things are very different over here. I mean with the sale of family properties and matters of that sort. Some of our lawyers reckon to be pretty good at tying things up, and there are more trusts and the like in our family than I'd care to count. But here these matters are still on a feudal basis, and a lot of your places are pretty elaborately entailed. I've heard that even when two generations see eye to eye in such a business a really strict entail can be hard to break.'

Miss Candleshoe now definitely reaches for the Madeira. Her own property, she offers, is an instance in point. Although not extensive, nor at all certainly associated with the Candleshoes until after the Norman Conquest, its tenure is believed to be a matter of the most amazing intricacy. Her brother Sir James – who reluctantly accepted the convention of knighthood on becoming Solicitor-General – used frequently to discuss it in her hearing with fellow lawyers deeply versed in conveyancing. Miss Candleshoe believes that if the property were to be disposed of there would certainly be a question of Crown prerogative. Moreover she positively knows – what is very vexatious – that she has mislaid the deeds of both home paddocks. But neither of these obstacles, perhaps, would prove insurmountable should sufficient – abundantly sufficient – occasion be presented for tackling them.

Mrs Feather, who is far from an artless lady, feels that this exploratory skirmish has gone far enough. As soon as Grant returns it will be time to bring the visit to a close. She gives her hostess a preliminary indication of this by picking up and smoothing her gloves. Miss Candleshoe, who is perhaps not an artless lady either, drops the stopper into the decanter and inquires if Mrs Feather is comfortably accommodated in an hotel. The Benison Arms at Benison Magna is said to be disagreeable, largely because flooded with sightseers, who are said to pay money to go gaping round Benison Court. Mrs Feather will recall that the servants of poor Dean Swift in his last years used to show their bizarrely demented master in return for half-a-crown. Miss Candleshoe confesses to a belief that showing one's ancestral home for a like consideration is an action of very comparable sort. But the Spendloves have not perhaps been at Benison long enough to develop any very nice feelings in such matters.

At this moment Grant and Mr Armigel return to the room. Mrs Feather, remembering the half-crown which she herself had been clutching in Miss Candleshoe's private chapel, has felt herself on the verge of blushing. She is therefore glad of the diversion. Grant and Miss Candleshoe exchange civilities about the injured part of Grant's person, which Miss Candleshoe roundly describes as a buttock. Mrs Feather gloves her left hand and rises. Miss Candleshoe makes Mr Armigel a sign which can only be interpreted as an instruction to ring the bell. Mr Armigel accordingly advances to the fireplace and gives a tug at a long silken rope, about the thickness of a ship's cable, that depends from the gloom of the ceiling. Perhaps because it is quite evident that nothing happens or can happen as a consequence of this ritual, Mr Armigel gives a second tug with rather too much vigour. The rope falls to the floor, together with a long coil of wire and about a barrow-load of plaster. The wolf-hound, which appears to be peckish again, falls upon the rope and savages it. It is apparent that the designed ritual has wholly broken down. There is no means of summoning a servant; in all probability there is no servant to summon; the visit of the Feathers to Candleshoe Manor looks like being, of necessity, indefinitely prolonged.

Grant Feather is rather disposed to turn and run. His mother advances upon Miss Candleshoe in good order, determined upon farewells. Whereupon Miss Candleshoe, with much formality and to the evident consternation of her chaplain, presents her visitors with an invitation to dine.

Mrs Feather has managed to get her back to the most recent evidence of the house's extreme dilapidation;

although the air is thick with dust and powdered plaster she contrives not to cough. She sees – being a woman of precise and rapid social discernment – that in the circumstances Miss Candleshoe's utterance is in fact less an invitation than a command. Hesitation must suggest a hint that the present resources of Miss Candleshoe's establishment may be severely taxed by an unexpected accession to her board. Mrs Feather has a very good idea how limited these resources are. Is she not, indeed, planning in the light of that knowledge? And here Miss Candleshoe is conceivably not without a fairly full insight into her visitor's mind. All this renders necessary the preservation of a very high decorum. Mrs Feather accepts – charmingly but without effusiveness. Grant must do something about their car – it can scarcely be left on the road-side while darkness falls – but that need take no more than fifteen minutes. Mrs Feather hopes that this interval will not conflict with Miss Candleshoe's customary domestic arrangements.

Miss Candleshoe is very clear about this. Nevertheless she will herself have a word with her housekeeper. Tapping with her ebony stick, and bent forward as if scanning the threadbare tartan carpet for an invisible pin, she moves towards the door. Reaching it, she turns and gives her guests a swift glance of stony irony. 'If there *is* a housekeeper, that is to say.'

She goes out. Towering over her, the wolf-hound follows.

# CHAPTER SIX

'As a matter of fact there is no housekeeper.' Mr Armigel, conducting Grant to the drive, becomes confidential. 'All that sort of thing became very difficult during the war.'

'The women went into munition factories, and so on?'

Mr Armigel looks doubtful. 'I don't know that I ever heard of *that*. But it was unsettling – decidedly unsettling. Women adore a red coat.'

'A red coat?'

'Precisely. You recall the relief of one of those places – was it called Mafeking? Both our cook and kitchen-maid, I am sorry to say, subsequently proved to have celebrated that occasion in a manner that cannot be described as virtuous. I remember reflecting at the time how distressed Colonel Baden-Powell would have been to hear of it. He cannot have intended that his gallant defence of the place – which was probably by no means worth defending – should result in lax sexual behaviour among the lower classes. You agree with me?'

'I surely do.' Grant sometimes encounters persons of mature years for whom 'the war' means a conflict beginning in 1914. Mr Armigel, going fifteen years farther back, takes him entirely out of his depth.

'Moreover two of our housemaids left soon after. Their lovers were hanged in the county gaol. It is an astonishing fact, but one well-attested in our poetry, that a high proportion of soldiers returning from the wars at that time *were* hanged in county gaols. But these girls were very upset, all the same. In fact they took a decided dislike to the district, and went away to places like Australia and the United States. We have never recovered – never *quite* recovered – on the domestic side. There is, as I say, *no* housekeeper. But at least there is a housekeeper's boy.'

'You mean somebody that runs about for a house-keeper who isn't there?'

'I ought to have said *the* housekeeper's boy – our late housekeeper's son.'

'Is he good with a bow and arrow?'

'Decidedly good. When our last shot-gun went – and it blew itself to pieces in my own hands, my dear sir, a circumstance somewhat alarming at the time – when our last shot-gun went, Jay developed considerable efficiency with a bow. At this moment I have a rabbit-pie in the oven – '

'Say, do you do the cooking?'

'Certainly. Jay and I largely divide the labour. He provisions the larder, and I make what I can of it.'

Grant considers. 'Is this Jay what you would call a strange boy?'

'Dear me, no.' Mr Armigel is somewhat anxiously emphatic. 'He is a very practical boy. We rely upon him in all our more prosaic and humdrum affairs. He could not, I fear, be called an imaginative lad, but he commonly has a sensible solution to any casual mundane exigency.'

'But he likes going about in fancy dress?'

'I cannot say that I have noticed anything of the sort. It is true that he is very good in contriving to dress himself in whatever he finds about the place, so his appearance may be a trifle outmoded now and then. I would not know. But I should not like to feel that his frugality in that regard was likely to lay him under any reproach of singularity with his fellows.'

Grant finds that Mr Armigel's remarks regularly require a little decoding. This slows things down. 'Then Jay', he asks presently, 'has fellows?'

'He has made friends with several other lads at the village school. Miss Candleshoe, who is fond of children, is very willing that they should play about together.'

'And fell trees?' Grant has remembered the obstacle laid across the avenue down which he and his clerical acquaintance are now walking. That Jay is responsible for it he has very little doubt. And it means that he cannot, in fact, drive the car up to the house.

'Certainly not! I am sure they would not dream of such a thing.'

Mr Armigel is shocked, and Grant sees that the situation is a little awkward. Because the tree has been neatly felled he is prepared to be on the side of the young wood-cutters. So Mr Armigel, who probably has not been down to the end of this drive for months, must be headed off. Grant has an inspiration. 'See here, Mr Armigel, don't you come any further. You have that pie to think of, and that's a whole heap more important than stopping along with me. I'll just get the car a bit up this avenue, and follow you back to the house.'

Mr Armigel discernibly hesitates. It is clear that part of his mind is indeed with his rabbit-pie. At this moment a twig snaps in the undergrowth nearby, and with the suddenness of an apparition the boy is before them. Mr Armigel is delighted. 'But here is Jay – and at a thoroughly apposite juncture, as is his wont. Jay, be so kind as to take Miss Candleshoe's guest to the lodge, and help him to dispose suitably of his conveyance. You will excuse me, my dear sir? It has occurred to me that baked apples, albeit an unassuming dish, may make an agreeable addition to our repast.'

Mr Armigel toddles away. Grant and the boy are left eyeing each other.

Jay is slim, straight, pale, dark-haired, and with dark eyes deeply set. He ought to have more chance of being handsome than attractive, and he clearly does not intend that his present demeanour should be held engaging. He confronts Grant grimly for a moment. Then he turns and precedes him silently down the drive. His bow has vanished, and he has changed out of his archer's clothes into very old grey flannel trousers and a dark blue shirt. Jay is long-limbed and will remain so. His arms as well as his legs move with precision as he walks. Grant finds it indicative of his own social inexperience that he would certainly have supposed this to be the young squire, happily bundled into his shabbiest attire for the holidays.

Grant overtakes Jay, but doesn't speak. He has decided that here is a nice kid, and he is anxious not to say a wrong thing. There has been sufficient evidence that Jay has no use for casual visitors to Candleshoe, and he wants not to get further in the boy's black books. They reach the felled tree. Grant stops. 'I've done a good deal of this in my time.' He steps to the tree's base and passes a hand appraisingly over the axed surface. He gives a curt approving nod and walks on.

Jay is looking at him sideways. The boy, he realizes, is not sullen or surly. He is wary – very wary – and now he is puzzled. He has put Grant in some category, and Grant's taking note of the soundness of the tree-felling job has thrown him out. But still he doesn't speak. Grant remembers that this kitchen-boy knows Meredith's 'Woods of Westermain', and this makes him steal his own sidelong glance. Their eyes meet for a moment and each looks away. Now comes the part of the beech wood, Grant recalls, that is curiously silent.

But this time he does hear something. It is the low murmur of a gently flowing stream. To the right is a small glade, and he can just discern a gleam of water. Something – to Grant no more than a shadow – flickers. But the boy has stopped in his track – and now he speaks.

'The kingfisher!'

'Could you tell, son, in this light?'

'It was the kingfisher.' For some reason the boy is darkly triumphant. 'That's always important, isn't it?'

'You mean lucky?' Grant is amused.

Perhaps he sounds so – for Jay flings round at him. 'Do you defy augury?'

So Jay knows *Hamlet* too. It occurs to Grant that Mr Armigel has been permitted but a partial view of this child. 'No,' he says soberly, 'I don't defy augury, son. And if there's good luck around, I hope it's coming to you. But what am I to do about my car?'

They have come to the ruined lodge. The dusk is soon going to give place to darkness, and there is something sinister about the mean, gapped building and the two piers of masonry and the single perched ball. It suddenly occurs to Grant that, so far as he knows, the only inhabitants of Candleshoe Manor are a couple of ancient eccentrics and this boy. And their situation is a very lonely one.

An owl hoots, and Grant senses Jay stiffening beside him. 'Don't you like owls, Jay? Are they ill-omened birds?'

'Anyone can make a call like an owl. That's why I don't like them very much.'

It is a quiet reply – but it comes to Grant with the effect of a flash of lightning. 'I can understand that,' he says. 'But there's the car.'

They turn down the road, and suddenly Grant is aware that Jay has skipped to the other side of it. 'Have you brought two cars?' The boy's voice is sharp, peremptory. He is like a grown man who suspects a trap.

'Of course not, son.' Grant peers ahead. 'But there *are* two cars. Now, that's certainly strange.'

A second car – another powerful American car – is indeed drawn up in front of his own. Two men have got out. They appear to be reconnoitring Grant's car – even to be poking about in it. Grant is indignant and surprised. Perhaps they are car thieves, but the spot is an unlikely one for that. It is an unfrequented road. A single glimpse of two cars standing together on it has instantly struck Jay as queer in itself.

Their footsteps have been heard, and the two men swing round. There is an uncertainty in their movements that betrays what is surely a criminal purpose. Jay gives a long low whistle on a rising note. This is promptly answered from half-a-dozen places in the wood. The effect is startling, and it startles the two men. They run for their own car, jump in, and drive off. As they go past, accelerating furiously, Grant tries to get a clear glimpse of them. But the light is too bad. As the noise of the engine presently fades, silence succeeds it. There is no sign of the children who have given this odd and effective demonstration. Nor does Jay refer to them. 'I can find you a way up to the house,' he says. 'It means opening some gates – and one or two other things.'

Grant for the first time notices the boy's speech. It is of the rustic sort, evolved through generations of slow thinking and slow utterance. But the boy uses it rapidly and nervously, so that the effect is markedly individual. Moreover beneath this or above this is something that strikes Grant as familiar. The accents of Miss Candleshoe and Mr Armigel are at play in the articulations of their young assistant. Perhaps it is only that. Remembering the rabbit-pie he looks at his watch. 'Never mind the gates, Jay. I'll just drive the car past the lodge and she'll be safe enough.'

'No.'

There has been a moment's deliberative pause and then the word has come decisively out of the dusk. Grant sees that on the kitchen-boy is some burden of command. It is perhaps from this that he gets both his pallor and his poise. 'You think those people might come back and take my car?'

'Your car will be better at the house. May I get in beside you and show you the way?'

It is a reticent reply, but Grant senses that Jay has made some important decision. He is quite sure that Mr Armigel's practical and unimaginative lad in fact leads a secret life of vivid fantasy, and that to this – or to a part of this – he has admitted some of his companions of the village school. Perhaps Grant himself is going to be approved; perhaps that is the inner meaning of the decision to guide his car by devious ways to Candleshoe Manor.

They climb in and Jay directs Grant to turn round. He watches as Grant's hands move over the controls. Grant realizes that Jay has the habit of learning all the time; that he could now, if necessary, have a fair shot at starting this car himself. He may get fancying things, but he is decidedly not what is called a dreamy boy. Grant wonders about his mother, the former housekeeper – where she came from, whether she has died or merely gone off with a lover, how the boy comes to be left apparently in Miss Candleshoe's care.

The secret route to the manor-house turns out to be a matter of traversing a couple of fields by cart-tracks and crossing the stream by a small wooden bridge. At the bridge Jay has to get out and perform some complicated operation in the darkness – a piece of ritual, Grant supposes, connected with whatever fantasy he is indulging. Once get such a fantasy going, he reflects, and anything that comes along will feed it. Two men driving down a country road see an empty car. They stop to take a rummage in it in the hope of petty theft. But for Jay and his concealed troop this drops into place as part of some vast shadowy adventure. Perhaps Grant and his mother drop in too.

The bridge is negotiated safely, and it appears that there is a clear run to join the main drive near the house. As Jay climbs back into the car an owl hoots again in the distance. And by way of experiment Grant quotes softly :

> 'Owls or spectres, thick they flee;
> Nightmare upon horror broods;
> Hooded laughter, monkish glee,
> Gaps the vital air . . .'

'*You* know that?' Jay is surprised; he has clearly supposed himself to be the only person in the world who has discovered Meredith's poem.

> 'Enter these enchanted woods,
> You who dare.'

Grant concludes the quotation and brings the car to a halt. The house, now dark and dimly sprawling, uncertainly towering, is before them. A couple of lights are burning on the ground floor. Their suggestion is of tiny areas of tenuous security scooped out of the void. Grant doubts whether, for a child living in such a place, imagination can be the most comfortable of companions.

'You got my message.' Jay has opened the car-door beside him, but for a moment sits tight. 'And yet you *have* entered, all the same. Do you think it was wise?'

'That depends.' Grant switches off his engine. 'If Candleshoe is like Westermain, I think I can take it. Dare, you know, and nothing harms. Keep your courage up, and fair you fare. I think I can manage that.'

'So do I. But then we are inclined to be boastful, aren't we? Or at least so Mr Armigel says.'

'We – you mean human beings?'

Jay can be seen shaking his head in the darkness. 'I mean people of our nationality – yours and mine.'

Grant bursts into laughter. 'Say, son, haven't you guessed that I'm an American?'

'Of course. And so am I.'

This is neither a boast nor a confession, but simply a piece of natural history. Grant is taken aback by it – the more so when he sees that he ought to have guessed. What in Jay's speech lies beneath its rustic and gentle components – the accents of his school companions, the accents of Miss Candleshoe and her chaplain – is Grant Feather's own tongue.

'Well, if this isn't a surprise!' Grant has taken to the boy, and now here is a bond. He is genuinely delighted.

'Even in England Americans must meet quite often, I suppose.' Jay remains objective and even cool. Grant feels on probation still.

They get out of the car and the boy produces a pocket torch. As he switches it on Grant tries a question. 'Do you remember much about America, Jay?'

'Nothing at all.' The beam picks out the first of the broken steps by which they must mount to the terrace.

'But you've read about it?'

'No.' The boy is abrupt. 'I know very little about it.'

They climb in silence. When they reach the terrace Grant speaks. 'Well – you've plenty of time. But there's quite a heap to learn.'

'I suppose there is.' For the first time Jay's voice is uncertain. It is as if he suspects himself of having been discourteous. 'You see, I don't really know much about anything.' He hesitates. He has reached the front door. He flashes the torch backwards to light the way for Grant. Then – perhaps the better to locate himself – he puts out his other hand to the smooth stone. 'Except Candleshoe. I know quite a lot about that.'

# CHAPTER SEVEN

THE rabbit-pie is a notable achievement, in point both of succulence and of mere size. Mrs Feather speculates on the oven from which it has emerged, and upon the invisible domestic economy of Candleshoe in general. She is obliged to conclude that there *is* no invisible domestic economy. The place puts everything on the table – and around it.

The surface appearance of the feast is that of somewhat rough-and-ready antiquarian reconstruction. Miss Candleshoe, it may be supposed, has formed a sentimental attachment to the Middle Ages, and like some eccentric in a novel of Peacock's has arranged her household, its usages and appurtenances in conformity with this fondness. She sits at the head of her board, with her guests on her right hand and her chaplain on the left. Her retainers sit below the salt. They consist of a good-natured and mentally-defective girl called Tib – of whom may safely be postulated an almost unlimited capacity for washing up – and a crowd of children. The children are a shock to Mrs Feather; she wonders for a moment whether Candleshoe is really a sort of orphanage, conducted upon lines which if surprising, are nevertheless conceivable in this perennially unpredictable country. It may even be an orphanage controlled by the State – in which case her cheque-book will be of no use to her. Grant, she sees, feels that he has a line upon the children; he is now more interested in them than in Miss Candleshoe. And in particular he is interested in the boy called Jay.

Jay is not at all suggestive of an orphanage. He has changed his clothes again – there is undoubtedly a streak of vanity in him – and is in black from neck to toe. Mr Armigel, if he sees this merely as a laudable economy, has become decidedly vague about immediate appearances. The old rag-bag stuffs suit Jay admirably; he looks like Hamlet in a cry of child actors – or might do so if his demeanour admitted any suggestion of the theatrical. When one returns to the medieval interpretation of Candleshoe one observes that Jay sustains the character of a page. He carves the pie and performs other menial services with the proper air of a lad of gentle breeding. Above all, he is businesslike. Like Hamlet he may dream. But like Hamlet he will be capable of arranging a very efficient Mouse Trap should the occasion for such a thing come his way.

Jay has a henchman in a fair-haired boy called Robin, who must be of about his own age. Mrs Feather guesses that Robin too has a good arm for a bow, and her ear tells her that he is not what Mr Armigel would call a village child – although it appears to be in the nearest village that he lives. Robin is the vicar's son, the doctor's son – something of that sort. There are three other children – two girls and a boy – and although simple they are unselfconscious and natural, which makes it certain that their present situation is without novelty. The wooden platters and pewter mugs with which they are provided enable them to eat a great deal of pie and drink quite a lot of what appears to be a decidedly heady brew.

From these utensils Mrs Feather's eye travels to her own. She has occasionally eaten off gold plate, but never off silver. The design is distinguished and she comments upon it to her hostess. Miss Candleshoe, whose head and hands alone appear above the level of the table, receives her compliments with civility.

'China of good design is hard to come by. My brother used frequently to remark that the Prince, had he lived, might well have elevated the public taste in these regards.'

'The Prince?' Mrs Feather is momentarily astray.

'The Prince Consort.' Mr Armigel takes upon himself

the task of courteous explanations to the colonial lady. 'We have been much grieved by his death.'

'It was untimely, of course.' Mrs Feather finds the tenses into which the chaplain is apt to cast his observations mildly unnerving. 'And I believe he was interested in the arts.'

'And crafts. But unfortunately a corrupt taste has become pervasive. Consider the novels of Lord Beaconsfield.' Mr Armigel pauses, but finding Mrs Feather without facility in taking up this theme returns to that of table utensils. 'As a matter of fact, we employed nothing but china until the Cataclysm.'

'The Cataclysm?' Mrs Feather supposes that Mr Armigel is referring to some obscure impact upon Candleshoe of the late world war. But she realizes that he may well be speaking of the Great Rebellion or the Norman Conquest.

'Tib.' Mr Armigel looks with great amiability down the table, where the half-wit girl is gnawing with concentration at the leg of a rabbit. 'She had not long been with us when our entire stock of domestic crockery vanished in one single act of destruction. Dispassionately considered, the feat was no inconsiderable one, since it involved the accumulations of some centuries. When we made inquiries about replacements, however, we found serious obstacles in our path – obstacles which might be subsumed under the two general heads of artistic and financial. Fortunately Jay – as so often – had a sensible solution of the problem. He raked about and found these rather older things. Upon their use, as you can conceive, one crucial advantage attends. The Cataclysm is impotent before them.'

'Was it Jay who thought of having meals together in the hall?'

Miss Candleshoe answers this, bringing her magnificent nose out of a fine silver tankard to do so. 'Certainly. The servants' hall was becoming a little difficult to use –'

'The river was coming in.' Mr Armigel interpolates this with casual pride. 'And the ceiling had come down.'

'Moreover' – and Miss Candleshoe frowns at her chaplain, conceivably feeling something impolitic in the suggestion that Candleshoe is in disrepair – 'moreover there seemed to be remarkably few servants in it. So Jay contrived the present arrangement, which works very well. I do not at all know what put it in his head.'

Mrs Feather suspects that the answer to this may be Sir Walter Scott. Being a woman capable of sudden large intuitions she has a sudden further suspicion as well. Unless there is a missing heir to Candleshoe who proves unamenable to financial persuasion, it is this boy who is the chief obstacle in her path. It is Jay alone who keeps the place going as a running concern. He has persuaded these old persons to revert, without their being much aware of the fact, to a feasible feudal economy.

Mrs Feather buries her own nose – which at present she is conscious of as rather undistinguished – in her own tankard. Mr Armigel watches her benevolently. 'You approve?' he asks.

Mrs Feather judges it safe to answer in the affirmative.

'Pears.' The chaplain is impressive. 'When lately we had some cause of – um – dissatisfaction with the wine-merchant – '

'A circumstance unthinkable' – this time it is Miss Candleshoe who interrupts – 'in the time of my brother Sir James.'

'And when, in consequence, we were under some apprehension that we might have to drink water – '

'An unhealthy practice – and, to my mind, uncleanly as well.' Miss Candleshoe disappears behind her tankard.

'In this exigency Jay evolved a reliable process for fermenting pears. The result is the perry which you are now honouring. Jay tells me that he has some thought of going on to mead. But that, it appears, needs bees.'

'Bees?' Miss Candleshoe is sharply interrogative. 'I saw several bees only this afternoon. Jay must be told.'

'I am afraid they belong to neighbours.' Mr Armigel is candid about this. 'Without at all knowing what may be the range or – so to speak – tether of a bee, I judge it possible that they may even be from the apiaries at Benison.'

'They were undersized bees.' Miss Candleshoe appears suddenly reminded of this. 'And their flight struck me as uncertain and sickly. Probably they *were* from Benison.'

'What you might call Whig bees.' It is Grant Feather who, rather to his mother's alarm, cuts in with this somewhat facetious remark.

But it is a great success with Miss Candleshoe. 'Our bees are certainly Tory bees. Or would be, if we *had* bees. Perhaps it is possible to breed them. Jay has had remarkable success with his geese.'

'He assures me that next year it should be possible to part with half the flock in exchange for a heifer.' Mr Armigel advances this as intelligence of considerable importance.

'An excellent plan. But the alternative advantages of several kids must be considered. A cow is very well. But while the cow is in calf . . .'

Miss Candleshoe and her chaplain drift for a time into problems of estate-management not of the first interest to their guests. Mrs Feather glances down the table, where something is happening among the children. Jay has given a nod – and at this Robin, the two girls, and the third boy have risen and are filing from the hall. A certain ceremony – or at least precision – attends their departure. It has, in fact, a military air. As they go, Jay and Tib employ themselves in fetching the baked apples, and for a moment the elders are left alone.

'Do you always have all those children?' Mrs Feather addresses her hostess with candid interest.

'The children? Ah, yes – of course they are friends of

Jay's. He has them to a meal from time to time.' It is evident that Miss Candleshoe, although her perceptions are still acute in certain areas, is a little cloudy about much that goes on around her. 'I believe the children assist Jay in various ways.'

'Jay, although not what may be termed an interesting child, has a certain organizing capacity,' Mr Armigel strikes in. 'His mother was the same. Without being in the least a woman that one would notice, she was thoroughly capable. We were sorry when something fell on her.'

'Something fell on her?' Mrs Feather is startled.

'Part of the house.' Mr Armigel appears to be surprised that there should be any need for this amplification. 'Miss Candleshoe acknowledged a certain obligation – the family has always done so in that precise exigency – and when no relatives of Mrs Ray's could be traced, she made herself responsible for the boy. He was still very small, and we had some thought that he might eventually work in the gardens.'

'If there *were* any gardens.' Miss Candleshoe adds this proviso.

'That decidely became an issue.' The chaplain nods. 'Jay sprouted rapidly, but the weeds were ahead of him. While the grass grew, the steed starved.' Mr Armigel frowns, aware of some lack of literary felicity in the application of this adage. 'However, Jay has now adopted what may be termed a wider sphere of usefulness.'

'Was it Jay's mother – this Mrs Ray – who was American?'

'Yes. It was a circumstance in which Miss Candleshoe took some interest, since she had at that time a nephew in Australia.'

'I see.' And indeed Mrs Feather has now learnt that from the Candleshoe point of view one outlandish part of the globe is much like another. Then a horrid thought strikes her, and she forgets all about her late compatriot, Jay's mother. 'Would that be a nephew who was himself a Candleshoe?'

'Certainly – a near relation. A little more perry?'

'Please.' Mrs Feather absently allows the chaplain to pour her out something like a further pint of Jay's beverage. 'And is the nephew in Australia still?'

Mr Armigel shakes his head. 'He passed on.'

'Oh.' Mrs Feather is a little ashamed of the manner in which she finds herself hoping that this is to be interpreted. 'You mean that . . .?'

'He was called to a better place.'

Mrs Feather sees Grant eyeing her satirically. She is genuinely contrite. 'Oh, dear! I am exceedingly – '

'California.'

'I beg your pardon?'

'He was called – or affected to be called – to more congenial employment there. It was always happening.' Mr Armigel pauses, as if in search of a turn of phrase which shall give the matter complete definition. 'Rupert Candleshoe might best be described as a rolling stone. Except indeed that his locomotion owed less to simple gravity than to traveller's cheques provided by his aunt. However – *de mortuis nil nisi bonum*.'

Mrs Feather can hardly trust her own Latinity. 'This Rupert Candleshoe is dead?'

'Certainly. His decease was obscure, but undoubted. And for the family it was, of course, a great calamity.'

'He was my sole heir.' Miss Candleshoe, despite some appearance to the contrary, has been following the conversation. 'As you will appreciate, this makes the future of Candleshoe more speculative than it has been for some centuries. Ah, baked apples! It is to be hoped that they have not forgotten the cloves.' Miss Candleshoe raises her magnificent nose from its near resting-place on the table-cloth to sniff. 'What is a baked apple without its clove?

Jay will no doubt serve them. I see that his friends have returned.'

It is true that several children have slipped into the hall. But they are not the same children who left it a couple of minutes ago, and their interest is not in the apples but in the abundant remains of the rabbit-pie. Neither Miss Candleshoe nor Mr Armigel is aware of this; to them one child is the same as another, and it is the apples that engage their serious attention. At another juncture Mrs Feather would take lively notice of this odd circumstance, and her son is certainly doing so now. She realizes however that Miss Candleshoe has reverted to serious concerns. There is no heir to oppose the selling of the house at an advantageous figure, and it is a course which the present owner is really revolving. Mrs Feather has been brought up in an atmosphere of business, and she knows by instinct whether or not a deal is authentically on the carpet. So she plunges boldy in. 'Candleshoe, I suppose, has never been without an heir before. It makes you feel that your own plans are unsettled?' She catches Grant's eye and feels acutely the indecency of such a question addressed to a woman who must be over ninety.

'My thoughts turn more and more to a very long journey.'

Mrs Feather's heart sinks. Miss Candleshoe, like the sick man in the play, is about to say with dignity that her plans are very simple and that she is going to die.

'In fact I am minded to embark upon the Grand Tour.' Miss Candleshoe proceeds with some briskness. 'Mr Armigel, I need hardly say, would accompany me. Moreover it has occurred to me that continental travel is always hazardous if one is unaccompanied by a personal physician. But a private chef is surely an unnecessary complication in the entourage of one who is happily free from digestive ailments. It would thus appear that the party may be completed simply by a courier and a maid; and that the Channel may be crossed by the common packet. But ought one to hire conveyances and horses at Calais, or take one's own? This is a detail which at present eludes me.'

'And you would go far?' Mrs Feather has no doubt that Miss Candleshoe would go far. But for the moment she can think of nothing else to say.

'I should begin with the Low Countries and proceed to some of the lesser German States. I have been told that the Court life there is frequently entertaining and instructive. I should then proceed through Switzerland to Italy. It has long been in my mind to view some of the scenes so affectingly described by Lord Byron.'

'We should then hire a schooner and proceed to Missolonghi.' Mr Armigel takes up what is evidently a well-rehearsed itinerary. 'Byron, poor fellow, died there, as you have no doubt heard. Our ultimate goal would be Constantinople and the monasteries of the Levant. There are reliable reports that it is a most interesting and informative part of the world. There was the Marquess of Dorchester's daughter – not, I think, the present Marquess – who married rather a dull dog, but nevertheless found Constantinople full of instruction. And I recall another lady of very respectable family who domesticated herself with Bedouins amid the ruins of Palmyra. She found them to be well worth a visit.'

'I'm sure she did.' Mrs Feather is a little taken aback at realizing that she may launch Miss Candleshoe upon a nonagenarian version of the travels of Lady Mary Wortley Montagu and Lady Hester Stanhope. Nevertheless she sees that the proposal has its advantages. Miss Candleshoe retired to a villa in Cheltenham or Bath is unthinkable; Miss Candleshoe lurking in some small dower-house on the fringes of her present territory might be a somewhat awkward neighbour; But Miss Candleshoe perched, say, on Mount Lebanon would at least be a monument –

and a blessedly remote monument – to the continued enterprise of her country and her class. 'I think your Grand Tour deserves to succeed. But travel, of course, is extremely expensive nowadays. Particularly with a chaplain and a physician.'

'We are under no illusions in that regard.' Miss Candleshoe favours her guest with an extremely penetrating if mildly lunatic glance. 'And particularly would it be so if we are then minded to move a little farther afield. There is an undoubted attractiveness about the idea of Cathay.'

Mr Armigel nods placidly. 'Perhaps you can confirm us in our impression that there is excellent sketching on the Yang-tse-kiang? Miss Candleshoe is fond of watercolour, and I still do a little in oils myself.'

Mrs Feather understands that China is indeed regarded as offering great natural beauties.

'Moreover it is said that fresh archaeological observations are still to be made upon the Great Wall.' Mr Armigel takes a pinch of snuff. 'I might conceivably address myself to a monograph on the subject.'

'An interesting proposal.' Miss Candleshoe is approving. 'Antiquarian investigation is a very proper pursuit to fill the leisure of a clergyman.'

To Mrs Feather it occurs horridly to wonder whether perhaps Miss Candleshoe and Mr Armigel are not already provided in some unobtrusive fashion with a physician, and with trustees or guardians as well. The English trade on being what Grant calls a mite crazy – of this they have had a sufficiently clear exhibition at Benison Court earlier in the day – but will even English social custom permit an old lady like this to dispose of property at will? May not some tiresome lawyer – or even Commission or Trust or Ministry – intervene on the ground that Candleshoe is a building of historic interest? But a building of historic interest is just what Mrs Feather wants, and what she considers herself very well able to care for.

She becomes aware that Jay is offering her another apple; she glances up at him and he looks her very squarely in the eyes. She supposes that Grant has made friends with him – Grant is wonderful with young people – and she is therefore surprised at something darkling in his brow. The boy has divined her full intention – she is suddenly sure of this – and his hostility to it is absolute. He is only a child, but he is the sole able-bodied and able-minded person about the place. He therefore bosses things. And he wants no change.

Mrs Feather takes an apple. At the same time, since she is a good-hearted woman, she begins to form romantic plans for Jay. He is a good sort of boy, with a straight if lowering gaze. For such a lad the concocting of perry and mead and the exchanging of geese for heifers is all very well for a time. But it is scarcely likely to lead to any very prominent position on life's stage. Jay must have education. Mrs Feather wonders whether it is too late to send him to Eton, which she understands is the best place for this purpose. But he can certainly go, like Grant, to Oxford. If he does well, he shall go into politics – British politics. Mrs Feather has not yet sunk her spoon into the fresh apple when the culmination of this reverie comes to her. Jay shall be Britain's first American-born Prime Minister. And when this happy climax is achieved she, Alice Feather, will present Candleshoe Manor to the nation as an official residence for holders of the office. Conceivably one or two such places already exist. But by that time she will have made Candleshoe so superbly attractive –

The undisciplined fantasy ends abruptly. For the second time at Candleshoe the Feathers are startled by the sudden pealing of a bell. This time it is from somewhere high overhead, and its character is not that of a summons to prayer but of a tocsin. The loud urgent clangour of the thing seems to crash down through the ancient building like a cataract and flood the hall. Jay drops his dish of apples and runs. The children at the farther end of the table follow him. Only Tib is left. The uproar delights her, and she laughs unrestrainedly.

Mrs Feather supposes that the place must be on fire, and the irony of Candleshoe's thus eluding her assails her vividly. She turns to Miss Candleshoe, whom she expects to see aghast, and who may well claim her succour on this dire occasion. But neither the old lady nor her chaplain are at all discomposed. Mr Armigel indeed has stood up and is reaching for the abandoned apples. The bell stops and he can be heard speaking. 'Jay's friends must have gone off to play at hide-and-seek. I am afraid they are a little noisy at times, but children ought not to be checked unduly.'

Miss Candleshoe nods in support of this liberal sentiment. 'Very true. And Candleshoe is an excellent place for sports of that kind.'

Mrs Feather supposes that this must be true. Voices can now be heard from various parts of the house, but they do not strike her as being congruous with a game of hide-and-seek. 'All these children,' she asks, ' – do they sleep here?'

'Sleep here?' It is one of the points upon which Miss Candleshoe is entirely vague. 'I hardly suppose so. But Jay makes his own arrangements. His friends assist him in various ways.'

The voices have now ceased and Candleshoe is completely silent. Grant Feather rises and slips from the hall. The bustle just concluded has spoken to him quite clearly. It has been occasioned by a garrison responding to an alarm and taking up its station. Hide-and-seek is no doubt a sufficiently accurate general term to cover the make-believe involved. But something prompts Grant to see if he can join in the game.

# CHAPTER EIGHT

BEYOND the screen the house appears to be in darkness, and Grant hesitates for a variety of reasons. By any standards it is a shade casual to quit one's hostess at dinner for the purpose of wandering about her mansion; and on this sort of thing it is very likely that Miss Candleshoe holds strict views. Again, he has really no business thrusting himself upon the amusements of this gang of kids. They have evolved, he can see, some large and sustained fantasy of medieval warfare. For them, Candleshoe is a good many centuries older than it actually is, and under the captaincy of Jay they are acting out imagined episodes of the Barons' Wars. There is no harm in that.

But may there not be the possibility of harm? A game played so intensely as this may turn, Grant knows, into a species of mass hallucination. And this tells him of another reason why he is thus hesitating in the darkness of the outer lobby. Let him once start groping about – a large dim figure discernibly not one of the crowd – and it will be scarcely surprising if some ancient mace or battle-axe is brought down with a crack on his skull. He remembers the warning arrow passing his head with no more than a discreet margin of safety that afternoon. Sooner or later these children must experience a misadventure. Their game, he has divined, has intensity as its hall-mark, and such violent delights have violent ends. This great mouldering house is more dangerous than a ruin. It is a brick-and-stone shell encasing tons of perished plaster and decayed timber – and the children go charging about it in the dark, bearing the actual weapons of its earliest time.

Grant laughs aloud. He would like to convince himself that he has lapsed into grandmotherly absurdity. But he is struck again by the queerness of the place. Its effective inhabitants are the children. Beside them, Miss Candleshoe and her chaplain are only ghosts – ghosts with a little grey matter still in the skull, but ghosts all the same. The children ought presently to be in bed – but who is to see to that? Besides Jay and Robin there are at least half-a-dozen of them. Presumably they all have homes in the village, and if they are found to be absent at ungodly hours rustic parents will bring to the irregularity the simple discipline of a strap. But there is no sign that the game is breaking up. Candleshoe is so quiet not because the children have departed, but because each is silent and tense at a station. Grant is sure of this in a general way, and as he himself stands taut in the darkness he tries for a more precise picture. At each end of the house a staircase winds upwards through a square tower; at the top of each there will be a ladder and a trap-door leading to the open air. Grant can see, as surely as if he had made the climb, an inviting intricacy of leaded roof, with that long scroll-work inscription by way of parapet. He can see a score of places where the finely cut stone has split and flaked long ago, and been cobbled up with iron bands which are themselves rusted away by a century of English weather. It is a wonderful eyrie, with vantage points at a score of places. By day – and even by night if there is a moon – one can command the gardens, the line of the drive and the stream, every break in the beech-trees, much of the farther country. And to sweep the terrace one has only to lean forward –

Grant shuts his eyes – and is aware of a play of light upon their closed lids. He opens them and sees that he is held in the beam of a torch. A moment later Jay and Robin are standing beside him; Robin opens what appears to be some species of dark lantern; and in the light of this the boys look at him silently. Then Jay speaks. 'Did you – did your mother – know anything about Candleshoe before you drove up this afternoon?'

'Nothing at all.'

The two boys glance at each other swiftly. This time it is Robin who utters. 'But you are very interested in it now?'

Grant shakes his head. 'I don't think I am. All you people interest me quite a heap – the things you like doing, and what you are busy about right now. But the place is nothing special to me. It's your place, I reckon – not mine.'

'But your mother wants it?' Jay's voice is at its most peremptory. 'She would buy it for a great deal of money from Miss Candleshoe?'

'Maybe so.' Grant tries to be easy. 'But nothing will come of it, I guess. My mother is always taking a fancy to buy places. But most times it remains just a fancy.'

'Do you want her to buy Candleshoe?'

'I certainly do not.' Grant is relieved at having it in his power to be unquestionably sincere about this. 'My mother is romantic, and sometimes she doesn't see how a thing wouldn't do.'

'A person ought not to come to a strange place without being asked and offer money for it.' Jay enunciates this rule of conduct with grave courtesy.

Grant, although not prepared to criticize his mother, feels unable to dispute the general proposition. So he says nothing.

'When a place is for sale – really for sale – boards are put up, and there are advertisements in the newspapers.'

'That's right.' Robin backs up his leader. 'And my father says only a lunatic would buy Candleshoe, because it's dangerous and unhealthy and inconvenient.'

'These are things which you should explain to your mother.' Jay is apparently unoffended by his lieutenant's revelation. 'And please say that Robin's father is a doctor, who ought to know.'

'And the place is haunted.' Robin is now eager. 'There

are two ghosts. And each is of a very specially terrifying sort.'

Jay seems at once to recognize this as a false cast. He silences Robin with a look. 'Probably your mother would like to buy the ghosts too?'

'Probably she would.'

'Ghosts can't be bought. It's a vulgar error to think they can.'

Grant receives this censure submissively. It is his inward opinion that Jay is right. The Candleshoe ghosts will in all probability not 'go with the house'. They are much more likely to accompany Miss Candleshoe and Mr Armigel to Constantinople or Crim-Tartary.

'May your mother be offering Miss Candleshoe the money now?'

'I guess not.'

'But soon?'

'She might.'

'Then don't you think you had better go?' Jay says this terribly quietly; he may fire minatory arrows at strangers, but he knows what it is to ask a guest to leave; he has strung himself up to it.

'Maybe we better had.' Greatly daring, Grant puts out a hand and gives Jay's arm a friendly pat. 'I'll slip out and see to starting the car. But as we'll have to go by the fields again, I'm afraid we'll need a pilot. Perhaps I could give some of your friends a lift home?'

The two boys confer in whispers. Grant remembers that the threat constituted by his mother is no more than an additional and unexpected danger at Candleshoe. Such as it is, it is a real danger; but in the minds of these strange children it is secondary to some more exciting peril of their own invention. It is on this that they are taking counsel together now.

'There is an enemy approaching the house.' Jay turns back and speaks in his most level tones. 'We have had a message flashed from our sentry at the end of the drive. That is why the alarm-bell went.'

'I thought it was something like that.' Grant is surprised to feel an uncomfortable pricking down his spine. The children's proceedings, he must finally acknowledge, cannot by any stretch of language be called a game. He is not in contact with make-believe, but with illusion – with fiction held as fact. He knows that learned persons would deny the difference; would declare that children are still playing when the suspension of their disbelief is entire; that they can be at once actors and spectators in a theatre where illusion is unflawed. But Grant feels this uncomfortable pricking, just the same. He would like to give the two boys a shake and say, 'That's enough for tonight.' Instead he asks, 'What sort of enemy?'

'We can't tell you that now,' Jay answers as he and Robin move through the lobby to the outer door of Candleshoe. 'But if we believe you when you say your mother won't really buy this house, and if we accept you as a friend, will you do something for us?'

'I'll do anything that doesn't strike me as dangerous and foolish.' Grant is guarded.

But Jay frowns, finding this a poor reply. 'It is dangerous.'

'Is it entering these enchanted woods?'

'Yes.'

'I said "dangerous *and foolish*". The woods aren't that. So go ahead.'

'Will you please take the torch, and go out of the house with a bit of a row when I unbolt the door? And then go and have a look at your car and come back – all in a very open sort of way? When you want to come in again you must knock' – Jay pauses and glances round him warily – 'and say *Christmas at Candleshoe*.'

'Is that the password?'

'It's the password for tonight. Will you do it?'

Grant nods. 'Sure. But what's the big idea – distraction technique?'

This puzzles Jay – but Robin gets it and nods back. 'I'm going out to scout around. I'll slip along the terrace while you attract attention to yourself and your car.'

'Very well. I'll start the engine and race her. Only, let's hurry – for my mother and I must honestly be off fairly soon.'

Jay whistles on a rising note. It is a sound Grant has heard before. Two boys and a girl glide out of the buttery and take their stance at the back of the lobby. All are deadly serious, and all are armed with bows. They stand with arrows notched, facing the door. The set-up, Grant realizes, is genuinely lethal. Soner or later there *will* be a misadventure. Jay has drawn the bolts. Before he knows it, Grant is outside, flashing the torch before him and whistling. The door bangs to behind him. As he takes a second cautious step down from the terrace he can just hear it softly opening again.

There is a clear sky and a sickle moon. After a few minutes in the open it would just be possible to get about without a torch. Driving will be pleasant – but Grant glances at his watch and wonders at what unearthly hour he and his mother will finally make a decent hotel. He wants to get away from this place. And, once away, he is quite sure that he is not coming back. If his mother really succeeds in bringing the crazy old dame to a deal he will go in and veto it. Once in a way, his authority with his mother will stretch to that. Let Jay run Candleshoe, hallucinations and all, until one morning its owner is found stiff in her bed. And then let family lawyers descend on the place and clear it all up. Let them, at a pinch, burn Jay's bows and send his forces packing and set him to a useful trade. It will be better for him in the end than getting the boundaries of fact and fancy so dangerously confused.

In this mood of impatience Grant comes to his car. He

climbs into the driving-seat and switches on a light. His mother's guide-book, with its fatal promise of long-and-short work at Abbot's Benison, lies open on the floor-boards. He picks it up and then switches on the ignition. He has promised to make a row, and he will. But perhaps he is no friend to the children in encouraging a mass of obsessive nonsense that has plainly gone too far. He tugs the self-starter. Nothing happens.

He tugs again – although already he knows that there is something wrong. After a minute he gets out, swings up the bonnet, and flashes his torch on the engine. One look tells him enough. The car will not move that night.

He finds himself acting in an extraordinary way. He flicks off the torch, reaches into the car and switches off the light, turns, and walks swiftly and quietly into shadow. It needs thinking out.

He has no impulse to suspect the children. This is intuitive and immediate, and only seconds later does he see that it is backed by logic. For the moment Jay is putting up with him, and has even pressed him into service. But the boy wants nothing more than to be rid of him – or at least to be rid of his mother. Jay has no motive for doing this thing. Moreover – ruthless as one may feel him to be – this can be guessed as something he would not do even to the most unwelcome visitor who had once received the hospitality of Candleshoe.

There is a possible explanation in insubordination and stupidity. Robin is certainly not a lieutenant to display either of these weaknesses. But there is a whole bunch of other kids, and it is unlikely that Jay has been able so to hand-pick his forces that one or two young blockheads are not among them.

Yet that won't do either; won't do for the sufficient reason that the job on the car has been a knowledgeable one. Grant begins to see why he is acting queerly. And he *is* acting queerly. He has got on the shadowed side of a yew-hedge, long since grown wild and cliff-like, and he is listening intently. He wants to locate Robin, now on his scouting expedition, and get him back to the house. For his own imagination is working. Just as, a little time ago, he could not bear the mental image of some tense child leaning far out over the crumbling masonry of the roof, so now he finds he can't comfortably take the image of Robin prowling these deserted gardens in a sliver of moonlight.

Grant tries to catch himself on a rebound from all this; tries to see it as darn nonsense. But the more he goes after such an attitude the less can he manage it. There must be some reasonable link between the extravagant fancies of Jay and friends and the hard fact that somebody has scotched the ignition of his, Grant Feather's, car. But instead of any reasonable supposition only rubbish comes into his head. The children are convinced that Candleshoe is beleaguered; that an enemy is closing upon it. Can a conviction like that, vividly held by a closely integrated group of young minds, set odd things happening in the physical world? A single hysterical girl is often pointed to as the source of poltergeist phenomena – of pictures falling from the wall and china hurtling across the room. Why should not a poltergeist of a modern mechanical bent get under the bonnet of a Packard and have no end of fun?

Grant finds that while his mind is spinning this poppy-cock his body is behaving with great deliberation and discretion. It has taken him silently to a gap in the high yew-hedge from which he can gain, as his eyes grow accustomed to the darkness, a faint but intelligible visual impression of a further reach of the gardens. The house is over on his left; the moon rides behind it; written as if with a heavy pencil against the dimly luminous sky he can distinguish in the balustrade a single Latin word: *Nisi*. Grant looks back to the garden. Out of the tail of his eye he thinks he has just caught a flicker of movement. He watches and is sure of it. Robin is flitting from shadow to shadow in a wide circle round the house. Grant breaks cover and goes in direct pursuit of him. At once his mind starts putting up a better show.

Suppose that Miss Candleshoe is a miser, and that the apparent poverty of her household is the consequence of this. Suppose she has mattresses stuffed with bank-notes and old trunks heavy with guineas and sovereigns and jewels. It isn't terribly likely, but at least it is a rational supposition. It is bruited abroad that to rifle Candleshoe would be to possess oneself of great wealth. Professional thieves take on the job. They reconnoitre the place – perhaps make some unsuccessful assault upon it. They lurk around, are seen in the nearest villages, withdraw for a time until any suspicions are allayed, return to further reconnaissance. And all this of cold criminal fact and intent collides with something quite different – the fantasy-world of Jay and Robin and their companions. Almost without realizing the change, the children have turned from engaging imaginary enemies to engaging real ones. And then –

Grant finds that he has fallen flat on his face, and that his face is most uncomfortably tingling. He remembers that bramble and nettle proliferate around him, and he proceeds more cautiously. Perhaps he should give a shout and summon the boy. It may be true that criminals surround them, but, even so, the best plan is probably to behave with the greatest boldness. In nine cases out of ten, surely, detected thieves and burglars cut their losses and run.

Following this line of thought, Grant is about to bellow out Robin's name when he remembers the car. It comes to him, obscurely but powerfully, that there is some sort of warning in it. Somehow the treatment it has received seems to speak of rather desperate villainy, and he wonders why. Jay would gladly be rid of the Feathers;

would like to see them trundling over the cart-track back to the high-road. Why should not the lurking criminals – if criminals there are – feel the same? If they propose to break into Candleshoe this very night, why are they not more than willing to see the departure of the evening's altogether unexpected accession to its garrison? There is only one reasonable answer. With one or two more people on the spot they feel that they can effectively deal. But they are taking no chances of the visitors' getting away with any inkling of what is going forward and the disposition to raise an alarm. Grant's car has been immobilized for the same reason that a telephone-wire would be cut, supposing Candleshoe to boast anything so new-fangled as a telephone: effectively to isolate the place while a projected assault is carried through.

Robin has crossed a stretch of garden already familiar to Grant, who recognizes the dull gleam of a pool and in the middle of it a patch of shadow that is the small crouching Nereid with the empty shell. There is a criss-cross of paths beneath his feet, but they are overgrown and in the faint light largely indistinguishable. The surrounding hedge, gapped and irregular, shows as a mere silhouette; it might be a scattered crowd standing immobile round some nocturnal ball-game. Through one of the gaps Robin vanishes and Grant follows. For a moment he distinguishes nothing but blobs of deeper darkness in a general gloom; for another moment he is startled by a sense of living presences all about him; and then it suddenly comes to him that his whole adventure must be a dream. It is a new solution, simple and comprehensive, and he is massively surrounded by evidence not otherwise to be interpreted. He has come to a halt beside an elephant; a hippopotamus is facing him; and beyond that looms a motionless giraffe. The forms are exaggerated and monstrous, but there is no mistaking them; his dream has brought him to a circus or menagerie, and in a moment he will wake up. Grant stretches out a hand to the elephant's trunk and finds that he is grasping leaves. He is in the topiary garden which – as Miss Candleshoe has explained – the children care for; they have transformed the shapes prescriptive in such a place into creatures that more engage their juvenile fancy. The notion of a dream must be abandoned. Here, in a special sense, is an enchanted wood, a grotesque metamorphosis of the plants. And amid these slumbering vegetable monsters or beyond them, it is his business to find the boy called Robin.

Grant advances. The creatures about him are mere roughly-shaped masses. But they are done with the sure sense possessed by children for the nature of material and for essential form; and in the darkness this makes them entirely alive. No doubt the obscure presence of danger helps.

> In the night, imagining some fear,
> How easy is a bush suppos'd a bear!

But here bushes *are* bears. Shakespeare slips into Grant's head only to slip rapidly out again – for suddenly he grasps a new fact. Endeavouring to follow Robin, he is himself being followed. He cannot tell by what sensory channel this knowledge comes to him. But he is suddenly so vividly possessed of it that he swings round like a man expecting a blow. Only the absurd menagerie is to be seen, its members standing improbably at gaze each with another.

Mythology has been admitted, for Grant finds himself looking at a centaur. The upper part of the centaur moves. It is some common four-footed creature, with a man slinking away from behind it. As Grant marks this, he feels a hand pluck at his sleeve and hears a low warning hiss. Robin, while making his own reconnaissance, has been keeping an eye on Jay's dubiously useful recruit. Grant sees that this is the situation, and he lets himself be guided silently from the topiary garden and into a narrow walk between high hedges.

'They've come, all right.' Robin whispers this grimly but with distinguishable satisfaction. 'We'd better cut back to the house.'

Grant agrees. He has left his mother to the sole companionship of childhood and dotage in what has turned out to be, really and truly, an unknown degree of hazard. The first thing to do is to rejoin her in the security of Candleshoe. For the house does, he feels, represent security – at any rate in some degree. It is a rambling and tottering old place, but he has little doubt that Jay has given much thought to constituting it a fairly effective fortress.

There is turf beneath their feet and they break into a run; at the end of the alley they plunge into a shrubbery and move forward warily. Grant guesses that they have rounded the house and are approaching it by the rear; he sees that, as they move, Robin is thinking out a route that shall keep them steadily in shadow.

He feels his arm gripped. The boy has come to a halt and is pointing – is pointing out into clear moonlight. Grant sees a small overgrown terrace beyond which the ground seems to fall away. On this a man is standing, facing away from them. He holds an electric torch at arm's length above his head and lets its beam circle slowly in air. The movement irresistibly suggests a summons, a command to gather. Grant likes it less than anything he has yet seen.

They have moved on, and a moment later the house looms before them. They skirt a wall, are in some cold, sunken place, have come to a halt in almost complete darkness. Grant hears the boy beside him tap cautiously on a wooden surface. A moment later there is a creak somewhere overhead on their left. He guesses that a window has softly opened, glances upward, and sees or imagines he sees the glint of an arrow-head, the gleam of a drawn bow.

'*Christmas at Candleshoe.*'

The words are breathed in darkness, bolts are drawn back, and he and Robin tumble into a flagged lamplit passage. Archers face them as Jay closes the door and shoots the bolts back home. Jay's pallor is greater than before; his lips are compressed; his dark eyes blaze with excitement. 'They've come?'

Grant answers. 'They've come all right – whoever they are. And now you must tell me, Jay. You must tell me the whole thing.'

# CHAPTER NINE

IT was the custom of Lord Arthur Spendlove when stopping at Benison Court to reclaim from time to time what had been an important privilege of childhood – that of climbing to the roof at sunset and lowering his father's standard from its staff. On our particular evening – for the narrative upon which we are enagaged will not carry us on to another – it was at a somewhat earlier hour than usual that he addressed himself to this mild ritual performance. The day had been a bumper one; they were still counting the stacks of notes and piles of silver at the turnstiles; presently a grand total would be arrived at and conveyed with some ceremony to the Marquess. From this and from the locking-up of the 'takings' – the word delighted his father – Arthur Spendlove found that he was willing to dispense himself. So he made his climb to the leads not long after the last *char-à-banc* had departed, and prepared to spend a contemplative half-hour with the face of nature as it appeared from that lofty station.

But from the roof of Benison the natural world shows much as does the Atlantic ocean from the deck of the *Queen Mary*. It is there – but at some remove, and with every appearance of respectful subjection. This appearance may be in both cases delusive; and Arthur Spendlove's consciousness of something of the sort made him frown as he glanced over the bleak immensity of Benison as this aspect revealed it. At some time or other an idle marquess had made a half-hearted attempt to ornament this sterile world of slate and lead, and had set up a proliferation of large stone objects – compounded, it might seem, from the mingled ideas of the urn, the acorn, and the pineapple – wherever an adequately supporting surface could be achieved. These meaningless embellishments, which a score of masons must have chipped at for a livelihood for months on end, jostled with chimney-stacks, skylights, trap-doors, and a complicated system of wooden ladders and guide-rails which had been run up for fire-watching purposes during the war. Round the perimeter of the building it was possible to take a brisk walk of just under half-a-mile, varied by occasional climbs from one level to another. This form of exercise Arthur Spendlove no longer favoured, but he did upon this occasion stroll some way down the east wing, pausing eventually to gaze with whimsical concern at a long line of concealed attic windows thus exposed. They represented the last addition ever made to Benison, and were just under fifty years old. For it had been Arthur's grandfather who, in a fit of eccentric benevolence, had presented his twenty senior maidservants with windows instead of skylights – and even with a bathroom to share between them. The windows remained, but the rooms behind them were uninhabited – unless indeed it were by ghosts too undistinguished to be mentioned to his father's tourists. Arthur liked to take a glance at these windows – forlorn and vain concession to the march of time – before turning to gaze at the unchanging lineaments of rural England.

He gazed now. The scene was not, after all, quite unchanged. Straight in front of him his mother's flourishing poultry-farm spread over the broad paddocks once reserved for the hunters. Since the western arm of Benison Wood had gone, more could be seen of Benison Magna – and there was more of it to see, a rash of small red buildings on the higher ground beyond the old town. Benison Parva had always been full in view; you could make out the village school to which his grandfather, in another spasm of democratic feeling, had despatched his father every day for a whole month – with a footman and a groom in attendance. Arthur Spendlove let his eye travel here and there. There was little ground, in the nearer prospect at least, of which he did not know every yard. And even in the farthest distance he knew just where the villages, the manor-houses, the farms lay. For a minute longer he stood beside the flagstaff, naming the places one by one. Kerpen House was still shut up : those people clung to London like Cockneys. You could see that old Colonel Riskey had given his little box of a place a coat of white paint. The gable east of the low church-tower of Abbot's Benison belonged to the house built by what's-his-name – a draper or ironmonger, surely, and now the local M.P. And on the other side, just distinguishable . . . Arthur Spendlove frowned, then chuckled. How ever could he forget that? Candleshoe, of course – the cradle of the family. He must ask his father if the rum old lady was still alive.

He hauled down the flag. As he did so he heard the hum of an engine, and went to peer over the apex of the great pediment immediately before him. One of his father's cars had drawn up before the main entrance and some-body had got out. A footman was hoisting a suitcase from the boot. Arthur glanced at his watch. Somebody arrived by the London train. There were half-a-dozen visitors at Benison already, and his father hadn't mentioned that another was expected. . . . He folded the flag, dropped it into its locker, and turned to re-enter the house.

Lord Scattergood was at the door of the small, strate-gically placed room from which he conducted domestic business. Seeing his son come down the great staircase, he waved a slip of paper in triumphant summons and dis-appeared within. Arthur followed and found that his mother was there too; she sat in a window-seat and was engaged in removing burrs from an Old English sheep-dog. Lord Scattergood again waved his paper. 'A very good day. Fifty-seven pounds fifteen shillings more than last week.'

Lady Scattergood looked up. 'Fifty-nine.'

Lord Scattergood picked up a pencil. 'Fifty-nine? I could swear – '

'Fifty-nine burrs on Brown.'

Brown uttered a low woofing sound. He was always gratified on hearing his own name, despite its humble associations.

'It's not bad going, even when you make deductions for wear and tear. And, of course, it is educative.' The Marquess seemed to challenge his son to deny this gratifying consideration. 'Lets one fellow see how another fellow lives.'

'Or lived.' Arthur walked over to Brown, disentangled an ear and tugged it. 'This creature', he said affectionately, 'looks more and more like a filthy old grey rug, with some appearance of animation deriving from the presence of unspeakable things crawling about beneath.' He turned to his father. 'You know that this game is all nonsense?'

Lady Scattergood raised her head. 'Surely not *all* nonsense, Arthur? In your father's ideas I have always been able – well, to feel something shining through. There has always been a *gleam*. Don't you agree?'

'Possibly so. There is something to be said for hanging on, without a doubt. In three or four years' time – well, one just doesn't know. Circumstances may change, feelings may change – and with them the whole drift of social legislation. Brown's day may be over.'

'Brown's day over?' The Marchioness was dismayed.

'Brown's and Jones's and Robinson's. It's excessively unlikely. But, as I say, one just doesn't know. So there is something to be said for living from hand to mouth.'

'I'm very glad to hear you say so, my boy.' Lord Scattergood was delighted. 'In point of fact, I have one or two plans maturing now. One of them is maturing here at this moment – I suppose in a hot bath. That is to say, if they go in for that sort of thing.'

Arthur looked suspiciously at his father. 'If who go in for what sort of thing?'

'Connoisseurs for baths. I've asked a fellow called Rosenwald for the week-end, and he arrived a few minutes ago. From Rome.'

'A man called Rosenwald has come all the way from Rome to spend a week-end at Benison?' Arthur shook his head. 'It sounds too like old times to be true.'

'There will be a small fee.'

Lady Scattergood was startled. 'You mean this man is going to *pay*?'

'Certainly not, my dear.' The Marquess was really shocked. 'We haven't gone into the hotel business yet, I am thankful to say. This fellow Rosenwald *gets* the fee. And his fare.'

Lady Scattergood parted the curtain of hair hanging over Brown's nose and gazed thoughtfully into the creature's seldom-revealed eyes. 'I should pay him only from Hamburg. It seems more suitable, with a name like that. And *why* does he get a fee?'

'For making an expertise.' Lord Scattergood was solemn. 'That, it seems, is the technical term. It means that he will find buyers for both Titians, and possibly for the two Velasquez portraits as well.'

Arthur Spendlove sat down abruptly. He possessed neither knowledge nor love of the fine arts in any marked degree, but he felt both startled and shocked. For a long time, indeed, he had been convinced that these and other family treasures should go. But the revelation that the cold wind of sober fact in such matters had at last penetrated the thick garments of his father's comfortable illusions was formidable. 'You've really made up your mind to sell?'

'Certainly. The right moment has come.' Lord Scattergood was very serious. 'It's much as with timber, you know. Or as it is with livestock. Recall how I found the psychological moment for parting with the Aberdeen Angus herd. I have an instinct that it's like that with Titian now. And probably with Velasquez as well.'

Arthur frowned. 'It's no more than so many square feet of canvas gone from the walls. But we'll feel it as the deuce of a gap.'

'Of course more must be laid down.'

Arthur stared. 'I beg your pardon?'

'It came to me not long ago that what one does with wine one ought to be doing with pictures and everything of that sort as well. Your mother must go round and pick things up. The same sort of thing, you know – but done by young fellows today. Nymphs and goddesses and portraits of big-wigs. We'll hang 'em up in place of the Titians and whatnot. And – mark my words, my boy – in a couple of hundred years they'll have matured out of all recognition. Given a century or two, the octagon room would do wonders for any picture.'

Arthur had heard his father assert much the same thing about the Benison cellars in relation to port. 'There may be something in what you say. But who is this Rosenwald, and how does he go to work?'

'He may come from Rome.' Lady Scattergood had her own problem. 'But is it from a shop, or from a museum? I mean, is he to have his meals – '

'My dear Grace, he is our guest – decidedly our guest. I understand him to be a private gentleman, who has become a great authority on his subject. I understand that he advises the Pope and a number of other respectable people who have these Titians and so forth on their hands. And his method of going to work is admirable. The buyer pays for the expertise. Rosenwald inspects the paintings – although of course he has seen them before – and then approaches his man. He explains that there is a chance – just a chance, you know, and extravagant hopes must not be entertained – that if he were authorized to negotiate with me – '

'I seem to have met expertise before – but I didn't know that was the name for it.' Arthur got up and opened the door for his mother, for a low-toned bell had begun to sound through Benison. 'It sounds as if the fellow will need a bath *after* the transaction as well. When does he inspect?'

'I thought we might all go up after dinner in a perfectly informal way, taking the Fernalls and the Crespignys and the L'Estranges along with us. It seems that Rosenwald likes these things to begin quite casually as a result of his having chanced to be stopping here or there with people of our sort.'

'What revolting rot.' Arthur gave the Old English sheep-dog a prod, and it moved shapelessly from the room like an enormous decayed chrysanthemum. 'What advantage can he get from a sort of charade played out before dreary people like . . .'

'Arthur, my dear.' Lady Scattergood was mildly reproving.

'Very well, Mother, very well. But Brown must come too.'

'Brown, Arthur?'

'Yes, indeed. Isn't he the last of us to know how to live with any dignity in this unfortunate house?'

It was early evident to his host – as also to the Fernalls, the Crespignys, and the L'Estranges – that Dr Rosenwald was a person of high distinction in the distant world from whence he came. He spoke with whimsical affection of the Pope, praised the claret, and described modestly but in some detail the little house – already a gem even amid the sequestered villas of the Brianza – around which, for the solace of his retirement, he was slowly creating a *giardinetto tagliato* in the antique Sienese style. Lord Scattergood, listening to this silken old person's evocation of the severities of composition involved, felt that Benison, where not a garden but an entire landscape had been made to order, must be a shockingly tasteless and extravagant place. The Fernalls, who were accustomed to spend a fortnight of the year with an aunt at Saltino, and who had several times under the superintendence of that lady surveyed the antiquities of Florence, were conscious of a just superiority over the Crespignys, whose acquaintance with the continent was virtually confined to the city of Paris and the more hazardous parts of Switzerland. Mrs L'Estrange, since she had artistic interests and was painted almost every year for the purpose of being exhibited at Burlington House, felt it due to herself to offer some remarks on Leonardo da Vinci. Her opinions, it turned out, were of quite amazing delicacy and penetration; Dr Rosenwald, picking them up as they were delivered – somewhat embryonically, it is true – from her lips, developed them into an elaborate and felicitous discourse upon *contrapposto* and *chiaroscuro*. This continued until the ladies had withdrawn, whereupon Dr Rosenwald, easily accommodating himself to the interests of the barbarians around him, fell to patronizing the port. Lord Scattergood, who had for some years been constrained to drink wood port except upon the very highest occasions, took even this in good part. As a salesman, Dr Rosenwald struck him as being incontrovertibly in the very highest flight. With an unwonted exercise of imagination, he pictured the excellent creature putting on just such a turn as this for some tremendous American millionaire – and all in the interest of the Spendlove pictures. It was in high good humour that he presently suggested picking up the womenfolk again and proceeding to the octagon room at once.

'Aha – the *salon carré* of Benison!' Dr Rosenwald struck his whimsical note, and at the same time gracefully accepted a cigar. Lord Scattergood, as a consequence of some odd upsurge of knowledge from the large school near Windsor, found himself wondering how *carré* could well described an eight-sided chamber. He perceived however that some compliment was intended – this sort of foreigner was always dishing out compliments – and he responded with the courteous hope that Dr Rosenwald wouldn't think the proposal an awful bore.

'But, milord, I am *enchanté*! This is a pleasure of which I not thought.'

Lord Scattergood saw Arthur gulping the last of his port and at the same time giving him a decidedly grim look. It was evident that Dr Rosenwald liked to play out his charade with an elaboration and completeness attributable – no doubt – to his large possession of the artistic temperament. Looking firmly at his son, Lord Scattergood inquired whether his guest might not, after all, prefer a game of billiards? Dr Rosenwald replied that the notion of taking a look at the pictures was a delightful idea of his host's, and one that he was altogether unwilling to forgo. He remembered them tolerably well, having seen many of them when they were on exhibition in London before the war. He assured Lord Scattergood that his collection was one, if not of the first importance, yet of very considerable interest and charm.

At this the entire party was presently reconstituted; a footman dispatched to switch on about a quarter of a mile of lights in corridors which it would be necessary to traverse; the ladies donned wraps – for even in summer the immensities of Benison could be chilly after nightfall; and the cavalcade made its sortie from the habitable corner of the house.

Dr Rosenwald paused to admire the Swedish Countess's sledge. Unlike the mortician from Buffalo, he did not apply a scratching finger, but sketched instead a graceful arabesque in air, presumably implying that thereby here was a formal assemblage of lines and volumes conformable with the nicest artistic taste. Lord Scattergood wondered if he was marking the outlandish old contraption down for offer to some hyperborean magnate in Greenland or Alaska.

Because Lord Scattergood had forgotten an appropriate key, the party had to pass down the long corridor that ran behind the main line of state apartments. It was crammed – as indeed were the leagues of similar corridors throughout the building – with the junk of three centuries of random collecting. On one side, in glass-fronted cabinets between the twenty regularly spaced windows, stood, hermetically sealed, sufficient china – much of it exquisite and most of it inconceivably hideous – to banquet the entire peerage; on the other were paintings, prints, statues, fossils, idols, flags, miniatures, enormous vases, fans, cannon, snuff-boxes, coins, medals, suits of armour, dugout canoes, travelling-libraries, geological specimens, and almost everything else that it is possible to amass. As Dr Rosenwald was delighted with all this, and remorselessly evinced the liveliest and most informed interest in the most outlandish of the exhibits, the progress of the party was on the slow side. Lord Scattergood wished that he had thought to put the cigar-box under his arm. His wife conversed alternately with Colonel Fernall and with Brown, neither of whom appeared to be in a communicative vein. Arthur listened to Mrs Fernall describing, in a powerful and resonant voice, her own wretched ill-health. The other gentlemen had fallen into a grave discourse of fowl-pest, hard-pad, and foot-and-mouth disease. Except for the exotic note struck by Dr Rosenwald, any stranger dropped miraculously into these domestic sanctities would have been gratified by an exhibition of English territorial life at its best.

At length they passed into Queen Caroline's Drawing-Room, and from thence to the Great Gallery. Dr Rosenwald stopped and pleasantly announced a modest desire to be shown the Cima da Conegliano.

Lord Scattergood glanced at the endless vista of paintings that ran in a double or treble line down the north wall and felt a moment of dismay. His librarian, Mr Archdeacon, knew something about these things – but Mr Archdeacon he had carelessly not thought to detain, and he would long ago have departed to Great Benison on his bicycle. The five-shilling tourists were uninterested in Cima da Conegliano, and Lord Scattergood was himself in consequence not as clear about this particular possession as he might have been. All the pictures here, he knew, were worth anything from five hundred to five thousand pounds apiece. It might be a good idea to sell the lot, and decorate this room with a nice line of mirrors. He seemed to remember that there was something of the sort at Versailles, a place at which the turnstiles clicked in a very satisfactory manner all day.

Meanwhile, perhaps his wife knew about this fellow Cima. He was about to inquire, when Dr Rosenwald fortunately noticed the Alessio Baldovinetti. On this master he had, it appeared, a difference of opinion with Dr Borenius, and he now proceeded to lay the case in some detail before Mrs L'Estrange. Mrs L'Estrange, gratified at this admission to the status of connoisseurship, offered intelligent murmurs. Her husband, who disliked what he called Kate's damned nonsense, made occasional growling noises indicative of impatience and distaste. Fortunately it was not easy to distinguish that these did not emanate from Brown. The party thus eventually reached the octagon room in tolerable harmony.

The stuff was all on one wall – the two Titians flanked by the two Velasquez portraits. For the two Italian pictures their owner had never greatly cared. As a boy he had judged them indecent indeed but unsatisfactory, since he had been unable to imagine himself in any amatory engagement with females of this species turning the scale at anything like the figure to be posited of these sprawling monsters. Later he had come to distinguish that they were what he called deuced colourful, but he had never kindled to them, all the same. He liked the reclining nude – she was said to be no more than a high-class tart, poor girl – better than the more elaborately engaged goddess hanging beside her. For one thing, he could never remember what that particular mythological proceeding was. And who had ever seen a swan of that size, anyway?

The two Velasquez portraits were a different matter. Here again he was bad at keeping names in his head – but he could accept each simply as a superb evocation of the aristocratic idea. This was even more true of the little girl than of the elderly grandee – although he was (Lord Scattergood suddenly remembered) King Philip the Fourth of Spain. Lord Scattergood had a great regard for ancient lineage, and admitted no illusion that a Candleshoe turned Spendlove in the later seventeenth century constituted anything of the sort. Now, therefore, he met alike the candid gaze of the little Infanta and the haughty stare of King Philip with a decidedly guilty glance. He was much struck, moreover, by the circumstance that

Brown had retreated to a far angle of the octagon room and sat down with his back to the proceedings. He suddenly decided that he would let Titian go, but hang on to Velasquez to the end.

Dr Rosenwald, with Mrs L'Estrange still beside him, was examining the Titians. At least he was standing in front of them, but it was not at all clear that they were very seriously engaging his interest. Dr Rosenwald's glance was idle, almost absent; and he was edifying his companion with remarks on some of the major private collections in Italy. Did she know the Bagatti Valsecchi Collection in Milan? Or the treasures of the Crespi Palace? Or the remarkable group of pictures assembled by the late Prince Trivulzio? When she was next in Rome – and, indeed, her so charming and cultivated husband too – would she permit him the pleasure of securing her an introduction to the Contessa Adriano-Rizzoli, who in addition to possessing a magnificent Quirico da Murano was also a lineal descendant (as Sir Max Beerbohm had pointed out) of the Emperor Hadrian?

The entire party – Brown still excepted – had now gathered round in silence. There was something undeniably impressive – even hypnotic – in Dr Rosenwald's manner of thus reviewing these major repositories of the plastic arts. Lord Scattergood however was impatient; he was, indeed, indignant. The well-cadenced discourse, the resonant names of noble families across the Alps, the eye so casually exploring the canvasses immediately before it : all these things had the effect of making Benison Court and its treasures seem very small beer. With mounting irritation Lord Scattergood remembered the price of a return ticket by air from Rome. And presently he could contain himself no longer. 'Look here,' he said, ' – what do you think of those Titians of ours? Are they worth anything?'

Dr Rosenwald looked at his host in surprise – as well

he might, since the mortician from Buffalo himself could scarcely have asked a question more baldly. Then his distinguished features transformed themselves into a smile – a smile at first brilliant, and then almost wholly reverent. He looked at each of the pictures in turn, and again his fingers traced – but this time with infinitely greater delicacy – their arabesque in air. 'Milford,' he said, 'they are a revelation.'

'Eh?' Lord Scattergood was startled. His guests were all staring.

'I had forgotten. Indeed, in seeing them amid the bustle of that London exhibition, I had perhaps not fully realized.' Dr Rosenwald was softly solemn. 'These may be – well, the greatest Titians in the world.'

'God bless my soul!' Lord Scattergood was almost alarmed.

'But *are* they merely Titians? I have to ask myself that. Yes, most seriously do I have to put that question to myself. It is the crucial point, milord, in the expertise.' Dr Rosenwald paused. 'And the answer I finally give myself is – Yes!'

'Ah – I'm uncommonly glad to hear it.' Lord Scattergood was now altogether at sea.

'But *are* they merely Titians? I have to ask myself assuredly, in the period – the tragically brief period, milord – of his supreme achievement. These are the work of the young Titian as he steps back – still dazzled and still divinely gifted – from the untimely grave of his exact contemporary and sole inspirer – *il miglior fabbro*, Giorgione!'

Mrs L'Estrange gasped. She could be trusted, Arthur Spendlove saw, to spread the tale of this impressive encounter with the higher connoisseurship broadcast among her artistic friends. And presently some young ass would be down from town, eager to do a talk on Titian's supreme creations for the Third Programme of the B.B.C.

Rosenwald was undoubtedly worth his money. Nevertheless Arthur still preferred the company of Brown. Brown, indeed, had a great deal of wool over his own eyes. But it was not his profession to pull it over the eyes of others.

Slightly dazed, the company presently drifted from the room. The women went to bed, and the men, accompanied by Brown, repaired to the smoking-room. Lord Scattergood took a stiffer whisky than was at all customary with him. It looked as if he might make out of Titian what he had calculated to make out of Titian and Velasquez together. The trollops from the Venetian *bagno* would depart across the Atlantic and the Spanish royalty would remain at Benison. There was in this – Lord Scattergood opined – a high propriety that put him in excellent humour; and he gave Arthur a wink – it was a bad family habit – over the heads of the other gentlemen. For a time Fernall, Crespigny, and L'Estrange lingered over their glasses. They had a notion that Dr Rosenwald, as their senior and a stranger, should take himself off first. But, the eminent connoisseur making no move, they eventually got up and went away, amid customary civilities and involuntary yawns. It had been a devilishly dull evening.

The moment was one for which Lord Scattergood – although with faultless dissimulation – had been eagerly waiting. He turned to Dr Rosenwald. 'Well,' he demanded, 'what are we likely to get?'

'For the Velasquez portraits and the Titians?'

'Just the Titians. Will they really fetch a notable price?'

'Undoubtedly.' Dr Rosenwald favoured the Marquess of Scattergood and Lord Arthur Spendlove with his most brilliant smile. 'Provided, of course, that you can find them.'

'What's that?' Lord Scattergood supposed that he had not heard correctly.

'It was a circumstance not very convenient to mention in the presence of your other guests. But the paintings now in your octagon room, milord, are not the Benison Titians. They are only copies.'

# CHAPTER ELEVEN

THE first to respond to this strange intelligence was Brown. He got to his feet and moved his mop-like head slowly up and down in the air. He had all the appearance of giving himself to an exhibition of well-bred mirth.

'Copies!' Lord Scattergood too had got to his feet. 'You mean we haven't any Titians after all?'

'Apparently not.' Dr Rosenwald was studying his host with interest. It might have been hazarded, indeed, that he was making an expertise. 'And I think, milord, you underestimate our difficulties. Still, something may conceivably be done.'

'Something may be *done*?'

'But no longer for what you call, I think, big money. So I hope you got a good figure – is not that the expression? – in the first place.'

Lord Scattergood's florid complexion had deepened to a colour which might have attracted Titian when looking for a nice curtain to hang behind a courtesan. 'Arthur,' he gasped, 'am I right in thinking that Dr Rosenwald thinks – '

'Probably you are.' Arthur Spendlove grabbed the whisky decanter and bustled about. 'But we needn't make anything of that. A damned odd thing like this may give rise to a misconception or two – eh? And no doubt Dr Rosenwald does meet some queer fish.' And Arthur turned briskly to his father's guest. 'Have another dash of this. All of us can do with it. Bit of a shock, you know. *Really* a shock. Just keep that in your head.' A man of more worldly guile than his father, Arthur thus steered deftly past an awkward moment. 'But I don't know that it's all that extraordinary. The war meant queer times for Benison, and a little large-scale hanky-panky may have crept in. Better send for Archdeacon.'

'Certainly we had better send for Archdeacon.' Lord Scattergood rang a bell. 'What about the Velasquez portraits – are they still the genuine thing?'

'Without question.' Dr Rosenwald had accepted with charming grace the invitation to apply himself anew to the whisky.

'And Cima What's-his-name, and Baldovinetti, and all that crowd?'

'Dear me, yes.'

'Well, now – somebody must have got in and played this trick on us. Or would it have been that girls' school?' Lord Scattergood was much struck with this possibility. 'The art-mistress, you know. I distinctly remember not at all caring for her. She might have done it at night.'

'Wasn't the octagon room a dormitory?' Arthur appeared not to think highly of his father's suggestion. 'And surely you didn't keep all those things on the walls?'

'Didn't we?' Lord Scattergood, vague on the point, paused to give an order to the servant who had entered the room. Then he resumed his speculations. 'Or would it be professional crooks? It seems a dashed queer thing for anyone of that kidney to take to. And how would they make money out of it?'

'Very readily.' Dr Rosenwald seemed now to accept the innocence of his host, and to be urbanely amused by it. 'I could tell you of a number of owners of works of art who have found it convenient to part with one or two of their treasures in an unobtrusive way. Do you happen lately to have inspected the Contessa Adriano-Rizzoli's Quirico da Murano – the picture I was mentioning to your charming Mrs L'Estrange? No? A pity.' Dr Rosenwald applied himself largely to his whisky. 'I painted it myself.'

'*You* painted it?' Lord Scattergood's indignation was

such that he had difficulty in articulation. 'Wasn't that a damned dishonest thing to do?'

Dr Rosenwald, by no means offended, raised a mildly deprecatory hand. 'Not, I think, *damned* dishonest. The purchaser of the original – he lives in Chicago – got very good value for his money, even although he is pledged not to exhibit the Quirico for twenty-five years. And what the dear Contessa is pleased to hang on her walls is entirely her own affair. Nobody is defrauded in the slightest degree. It is not as if she made visitors to the Palazzo Rizzoli pay at the door.' And leaving Lord Scattergood to digest this as he might, Dr Rosenwald turned to Arthur. 'Excuse me,' he said, 'I am interested. Does this whisky come from Scotland or from Ireland?'

Reminding himself that Dr Rosenwald was his guest, Lord Scattergood took a turn about the room. 'Would you mind telling me', he said presently, 'how long it would take to concoct these two things now passing as my Titians?'

Dr Rosenwald considered. 'I think it likely', he said, 'that I could manage one in three months.'

'Bless my soul!' It had never occurred to Lord Scattergood that any work of art, whether authentic or spurious, could take more than three or four days to execute. 'What a deuced odd way for a fellow to spend his time! I can remember doing art at my private school. But it never went on for more than fifty minutes. And the last ten of those were commonly a bit of a rag.'

'Surely those Titians are insured?' Arthur halted his father's irrelevance by asking this question abruptly. 'If they are, this outrage at least isn't dead loss.'

'A very interesting point.' Benignly smiling, Dr Rosenwald shook a richly experienced head. 'Let us hope, by all means, that they are insured. But, you know, the insurance people will fight.'

'Why the dickens should they fight?'

'My dear Lord Arthur, they will fight because of the magnitude of the sum involved. They will take you to – what do you call it? – the House of Lords. They will take you to – am I right? – the Judicial Committee of your Privy Council. If, that is to say, it is necessary to fight in more than one court.'

Arthur frowned. 'I don't see that they'd have a leg to stand on.'

'On the contrary. Your father, I fear, may have great difficulty in establishing that he has ever been the owner of two authentic Titians. For an unknown length of time, two modern paintings have been hanging in Benison Court; and it has been represented – and of course believed – by the Marquess of Scattergood that these were authentic works. We cannot explain, or put an exact date to, the supposed substitution. The position, believe me, my dear Lord Arthur, is a difficult and delicate one.' Dr Rosenwald drained his glass. 'And now, milord, we had better return to the octagon room.'

'Certainly – if you think it any good.' Lord Scattergood was impressed by something businesslike that either the whisky, or the present exigency, or both, had begun to induce in the deplorable visitor from Rome. He moved to the door and looked at his watch. 'My librarian and curator, Mr Archdeacon, should be here in half-an-hour. I sent a car. Perhaps I should tell you' – and Lord Scattergood looked at his guest with some severity – 'that in addition to being extremely learned, and everything of that sort, he is a very old friend of the family.'

Dr Rosenwald made a graceful motion with a hand that had somehow managed to get hold of another cigar. 'Mr Archdeacon', he said suavely, 'is a scholar whom I have long been anxious to meet.'

Attended only by Brown, the three men returned in silence through the long empty corridors. And presently they were once more facing the spurious progeny of

Tiziano Vecellio. Dr Rosenwald, who had so edified Mrs L'Estrange by his ecstasies before them half an hour ago, shook an unblushing head. 'So-so,' he said. 'Decidedly so-so. It surprises me that no moderately-informed visitor – But no matter. I think we will have the Leda, if you please, down from the wall.'

'Is that the one with the swan?' Lord Scattergood looked at the picture with a distaste only intensified by his new knowledge. 'I've never had any notion of what it's about, and I wouldn't like to mention the idea it puts in my head. Had we better have a man up to help?'

'Much better not. Lord Arthur and I will have no difficulty.' Dr Rosenwald was a monument of discretion. 'These little troubles, believe me, are sometimes best kept in the family.'

Arthur, remarking his father compress his lips at the promotion which this smooth old rascal was thus according himself, made haste to get to work on the canvas. They lowered it to the floor. Dr Rosenwald, producing a magnifying-glass and an instrument like a scalpel, took on an air of professional intentness that was undeniably impressive. He might have been a plastic surgeon in fashionable practice, and about to address himself to Leda's rotundities in the interest of a modern *couture*. Or he might have been a poulterer, minded to prepare her web-footed friend for some traditional feast. His actual proceedings, however, amounted to no more than first taking a glance at the back of the canvas and then doing a certain amount of scratching and scraping of its painted surface. Lord Scattergood watched him uneasily. There had come into his head the alarming idea that Dr Rosenwald might be either a madman or a monstrous practical joker, and the work he was thus chipping at an authentic masterpiece of the sixteenth century after all.

But any such notion as this evaporated before the brisk conviction with which the eminent Roman connoisseur presently straightened himself and spoke. 'There is no question of what you would call a fake. The work has been done on a new canvas, not an old one. And the pigments and processes are palpably modern. This is not a forgery. There has been no attempt to deceive an expert.' Dr Rosenwald spoke as one frankly disappointed that the higher levels of his science need not be called into play. 'This is a straightforward copy, and nothing else.'

'The sort of thing you see old ladies doing in the National Gallery and all those places abroad?' Lord Scattergood seemed mildly surprised at the reach of his own artistic information.

'Precisely that sort of thing. And I see no need for a more particular examination of the other painting at present.'

'You're quite sure that it's all right about Velasquez?' Lord Scattergood exchanged an uneasy glance with King Philip and the Infanta. It appeared altogether shocking to him to have to ask such a question in their presence. But his anxiety forbade him to wait until he was once more out of their view. 'Hadn't you better vet them a little more thoroughly?'

Dr Rosenwald shook his head. 'Your Velasquez portraits are authentic. On Velasquez, milord, I could not be deceived in the dark. On Velasquez' – and Dr Rosenwald brilliantly but modestly smiled – 'I am the first authority in Europe.'

The arrival of Mr Archdeacon in the smoking-room some fifteen minutes later was distinguished by a demonstration on the part of Brown. The high regard which the Spendlove family in general felt for their librarian was clearly shared by this severer judge. He and Mr Archdeacon, in fact, embraced cordially; and as Mr Archdeacon was a venerable person with flowing white hair, abundant eyebrows, and a bushy beard the visual effect was striking. It was some moments before Lord Scattergood could provide the new arrival with whisky and introduce Dr Rosenwald. He then explained the state of the case. Listening in silence, Mr Archdeacon occupied himself with stuffing an enormous pipe.

'So you see, my dear Archdeacon, here is a shocking thing. I can't imagine anything more disgraceful. We have been showing these pictures to the public as being by Titian, and it turns out that they are by somebody quite different – a school-mistress perhaps, or a new sort of burglar.'

Mr Archdeacon nodded through a cloud of smoke. 'It is very deplorable, to be sure. But beauty, after all, is in the eye of the beholder.'

'Is that so? I hadn't heard.' Lord Scattergood received this mysterious intelligence respectfully. 'And that makes a difference?'

'Assuredly. Let us conclude that each man largely creates the beauty he experiences, and our position is morally a strong one. Let me be very clear, very simple. By "Titian" – or shall we say rather by "Titianness"? – we mean a class of experiences, preponderantly emotional but in part intellectual, varying from individual to individual within limits which I shall presently endeavour to define. "Titianness", in fact, is a term only applicable with any philosophical strictness to phenomena of a purely subjective character. Whether that in the outer world whereby the response of "Titianness" is occasioned has or has not any objective and verifiable connexion with the man Tiziano Vecellio is a circumstance altogether immaterial.' Mr Archdeacon emitted a further cloud of smoke, which had perhaps the effect of a little obscuring his train of thought. 'So, you see, we need not really worry on the score of having been parties to a deception.'

'I'm extremely glad to hear it.' Lord Scattergood's gratitude to the family sage for this clarification of his ethical position was unaffected. 'I was afraid, you see, that we hadn't been giving people their money's worth. Forgeries, after all, are not at all a nice thing to have about.'

'My dear Marquess, we are all forgeries.'

'You don't say so!'

'Certainly – even Brown.' From behind his now impenetrable cloud Mr Archdeacon gave a Jehovah-like chuckle. 'Brown himself is but a counterfeit, a feeble copy of the real Brown – whom we should find, you know, only in the kennels of Heaven. And were Titian – or shall we say the late Sir Edwin Landseer? – to execute a painting of our Brown, what would this be but a copy of a copy, a shadow of a shadow? Now, suppose further that a forger gets to work on Landseer's painting. His work will be at but one further remove from the real Brown – the shadow, we may say, of a shadow's shadow. There is here a field for abundant reflection.'

'That's extremely true.' Lord Scattergood hesitated before descending from these edifying and Platonic heights. 'But the plain fact, my dear fellow, is this: that people who collect art and so forth don't manage to take your profound sort of views. They have matter-of-fact minds, Archdeacon – damned matter-of-fact minds. And the disappearance of these things means that I stand to lose the deuce of a lot of money. To tell you the truth, Dr Rosenwald here was going to find a millionaire or two to take the Titians off my hands for an uncommonly large sum.'

'That's another matter.' Abruptly Mr Archdeacon rose to his feet and emerged from the layers of smoke wherein he had been enshrouded. 'The paintings must be recovered.' He turned to Dr Rosenwald. 'When, pray, would the copies have been executed?'

'Judging from the state of the pigment, they are not less than three years old, and not more than ten.'

'You are sure of that?'

'My good sir, with me these are matters of professional knowledge.' Dr Rosenwald was gracefully magistral. 'I have no doubt of it whatever.'

'Very good.' Mr Archdeacon, who had taken upon himself with surprising suddenness the role of practical investigator, paused to give Brown an amiable cuff on the nose. 'And now be so good, Dr Rosenwald, as to tell me this: is it possible, in your judgement, that these copies could have been made other than direct from the originals? I may remind you that the Marquess many years ago gave permission for the preparation and sale of colour prints of a superior sort, and that the paintings have further been photographed in considerable detail.'

Dr Rosenwald considered. 'The copies are not very good copies. But they have been executed with much care, and almost certainly from the originals. And that would involve access to the originals covering a period of many weeks – probably, indeed, of many months.'

'Thank you.' Mr Archdeacon, accompanied by Brown, took a turn about the room. Both Lord Scattergood and his son watched the family oracle respectfully. Dr Rosenwald benefited by their absorption to the extent of a further glass of whisky and a third cigar. 'There can be no doubt as to how the matter stands.' Mr Archdeacon came to a halt again before his employer. 'Unfortunately it can only be described as in a posture of some delicacy.'

'Is that so?' Lord Scattergood was dismayed. 'And you don't see quite what to do?'

'I by no means make that asseveration.' Having delivered himself of this mild rebuke, Mr Archdeacon briefly resumed his perambulation. For a moment he halted in a far corner – seemingly for the purpose of conferring with Brown. And presently he returned. 'You will recall that at the outbreak of war we sent a good many of the things away. With so important a Ministry proposing to move in, it looked as if we might well be singled out as a target for aerial attack.'

'To be sure.' Lord Scattergood nodded intelligently. 'I remember that you advised sending the muniments to Corbies.'

'They were, of course, the objects of our chief concern.' Mr Archdeacon turned to Dr Rosenwald. 'Paintings and so forth are one thing. But family documents, I am sure you will agree, are quite another.'

Whether the eminent connoisseur indeed concurred in the view that charters and title-deeds must enjoy priority over the achievements of Cima da Conegliano and Alessio Baldovinetti – let alone of Titian and Velasquez – was highly doubtful. Dr Rosenwald however had by this time advanced so far in independent research into the territorial origins of Lord Scattergood's whisky as to be indisposed to argument on the subject; so that Mr Archdeacon presently resumed his observations to the room in general.

'But we did at the same time disperse a considerable number of the works of fine art – the major Italian and Spanish paintings included. It was not easy, however, to arrange transport to Scotland on a large scale. I bethought myself, therefore, of invoking the courtesy of our more retired neighbours. That Benison should be bombed appeared not improbable. But who would wish, for example, to blow up old Colonel Riskey?'

Lord Scattergood nodded. 'Very true. Unless one knew him, that is to say. And he had probably never run up against Goering and those fellows personally.'

'Or what likelihood was there of enemy action being directed upon an edifice so inconsiderable as Kerpen House?' Mr Archdeacon paused. 'So I sent the better ceramics and bronzes to Sir Richard, and the Colonel was good enough to house the prints and drawings.'

'And the paintings?' Lord Scattergood was all anxiety. 'It was in them, after all, that the hard cash lay.'

'Precisely. The point had by no means escaped me.' For a moment or two Mr Archdeacon applied himself once more to his pipe. 'I therefore arranged that the paintings should go to the most retired and insignificant spot of all. Or insignificant, I should say, but for the accident of its early association with the family. In short . . .'

'Candleshoe!' Understanding flashed upon Lord Scattergood. 'The paintings went there?'

'The most important paintings certainly did. And at Candleshoe, clearly, the substitution must have been effected.'

'Then we must go and find out. I'll order round a car this minute.' And Lord Scattergood firmly rang a bell for the second time that evening. 'But – by Jove! – isn't the old lady said to be a bit hard to handle?'

'There is not a doubt of it. Only the high vein of patriotic feeling current at that time disposed her, if I recollect rightly, to admit anything at all from Benison. And she charged a good round figure, too.' Lord Scattergood's philosophic librarian took another puff at his pipe. 'Fortunately it occurred to me to send on the bill to the Ministry. They paid, without demur.'

Arthur Spendlove was looking doubtful. 'Ought we really to go over there at this hour? We can't ring up and make a civil inquiry about its being convenient. Candleshoe is certainly not on the telephone.'

'It might be described as only very uncertainly on the map.' Mr Archdeacon was on the point of indulging himself in a laugh on the strength of this witticism, but was dissuaded by an evidently disapproving gesture on the part of Brown. 'It makes, that is to say, no great figure in the world at present. I doubt whether there be anybody there except Miss Candleshoe herself – unless, indeed, she still has poor Armigel.' And Mr Archdeacon shook his venerable locks. 'The dear old boy must be getting on.'

Lord Scattergood looked at his watch. 'Perhaps, after

all, it would be better to wait till the morning? A spinster of advanced years, don't you know, living in a tumbledown place like that, might be a bit alarmed – '

'I think we'd better go now.' Arthur had changed his mind. 'If there is really some danger of the old lady's being uncooperative, something in the way of shock tactics may be the best start.'

'Very true, my dear boy – very true, indeed.' With some dexterity, Lord Scattergood moved the whisky decanter out of Dr Rosenwald's immediate reach. 'Not that I'd want to do anything to upset old Miss Candleshoe. We've none of us seen her for years, you know; and I have an idea that she has a bit of a bee in her bonnet in the matter of the family history. Absurd – but there it is. And I shouldn't be surprised if she's in difficulties. I think it very possible that she's hard up. Shocking to think of – eh?' Lord Scattergood was genuinely distressed at the notion of indigence among the upper classes. 'But we'd better be off at once. Arthur, will you drive? No need to drag out Ball. Archdeacon, my dear fellow, I rely on you to come along. Fortunately it's a mild night, and there will be a bit of a moon.' Lord Scattergood's eye, as he spoke, fell upon Dr Rosenwald. 'Good lord – is that fellow asleep?'

Arthur gave the connoisseur an unceremonious prod – without discernible effect. 'Heavily, it seems. Perhaps he's unused to whisky – eh?'

'Had we better rouse him and take him along?' Lord Scattergood consulted his librarian. 'Would he be useful with the old girl?'

The sage nodded. 'Not perhaps with the old girl – but conceivably with the Old Master.'

'What's that? James Candleshoe died years ago.'

'You misapprehend me, my dear Marquess. I refer to Titian.'

'To be sure. And what a deuced mysterious business

this is! But I believe, my dear Archdeacon, that you already see some light in it.'

The librarian, who was re-enveloping himself in an ancient Inverness cape, paused to consider this. 'I think I may say that I see some possibility of presently advancing upon a working hypothesis.'

'By jove! is that so?' Lord Scattergood was impressed. 'Had I better bring a gun?'

'My dear Marquess, all we need take is authority and a clear head. It is a situation in which we ought to have no difficulty in effecting a convenient division of labour.'

# CHAPTER TWELVE

CANDLESHOE has ample cellarage, and parts of this are distinguishably of far greater antiquity than is the house. It is supposed that when Robert Candleshoe built his ambitious new dwelling he incorporated in its foundations the substructure of some immemorial building acquired by the family upon its first coming to prosperity. It is here only that the ghosts walk – a circumstance which would seem to argue the very high antiquity of these apparitions. There can be little doubt that the ghosts look upon Candleshoe as Candleshoes look upon Spendloves. When these spirits were incarnate, William of Normandy had not yet come to England.

It is at this lower level that Grant Feather and the boy Robin have been readmitted to the beleaguered house. The children themselves are as pale as ghosts. But Jay, who leads them, is less like a ghost than a flame. Crisis has come, and he has kindled to it.

Grant now realizes that the place is actually under some sort of threat from an unknown number of rascals gathered outside it. These can hardly be intending assault and violence for its own sake. They can scarcely, for instance, be prosecuting any species of blood-feud with Miss Candleshoe or old Mr Armigel. Robbery must be their motive – although it is hard to see what in this poverty-stricken mansion can be worth removal. Still, theft alone can be their object; and this is a circumstance slightly alarming perhaps, but prosaic enough. Over against it is the other and disproportionate fact of these children's emotional state, of their dangerous weapons and resolute bearing; of an exaltation in their leader for which Grant obscurely feels there is an ominous word. He is acutely conscious that the situation must be controlled. Fate, in tumbling him into Candleshoe on this particular evening, seems to have handed him out this assignment and to be watching with an unwinking eye how he measures up to it. Grant walks up to Jay, puts a hand on his shoulder, and repeats what he has just said. 'You must tell me the whole thing.'

'Come upstairs.' This from Jay may be either a request or an order. The boy speaks rapidly to Robin – he seems constantly to be redisposing the small force at his command – and then turns and strides away. Grant follows. It is a narrow passage, stone-vaulted and flagged, and their foot-falls have an exaggerated resonance, like an effect for radio. Jay carries a lantern; its light glints on something richly figured in the outlandish old clothes which he wears with so sombre a grace. 'Fey' is the ominous word that might be applied to the boy; it is conceivable that as the climax of this nonsense he is expecting to die.

Grant feels the necessity of saying something commonplace. 'Jay,' he asks, 'what's my mother doing? I'd better have a word with her and explain how we're held up. And Miss Candleshoe will be wondering why we don't clear out.'

'The women must wait.' Jay makes this pronouncement without turning round, but as they are now ascending a spiral stone staircase his features are just visible in profile, lit up from below by the lantern he carries at his knee. Seen thus, he looks calmer and older; desperate as the situation may be, he is conscious of having a masculine grip on it; the words he has just spoken come from him perfectly naturally.

Grant reflects that his mother has little sense of time, Miss Candleshoe much less, and Mr Armigel demonstrably none at all. He had better not bother about them, therefore, until he has won Jay's confidence – as there seems at least to be a chance of doing. They have emerged on the ground floor, crossed a lobby, and are now climbing a broader staircase with shallow wooden treads. It goes up and up by short flights round a rectangular well, and on several landings they pass without pausing high closed doors that must give upon apartments of consequence long ago. The perishing timber creaks beneath their feet; dust lies on the dull surfaces of ancient chests and cupboards in the window-embrasures; thick dust swims in the beam of Jay's lantern. The whole place smells of decay – of the slow inoffensive decay of dry panelling and crumbling leather and tindery hangings and innumerable stuffs and fabrics long since laid carefully away.

A slight sound behind Grant makes him whirl round in a flash. There is nothing there except his old antagonist the wolf-hound. Jay turns too. 'Don't mind Lightning – even if he did take a nip at you before. He usually follows me round.'

'Certainly I shan't mind Lightning.' Grant realizes from the speed of his own reaction how much he is keyed-up. 'Are we going right to the roof?'

'No – only to the gallery. If you are to know, you may as well be shown, I think.' Suddenly Jay stops, turns, and raises the lantern high in air, so that Grant is full in the light of it. 'Do you give me your word that you haven't come here because you *do* know?'

'I didn't come here as a result of knowing anything, Jay. My mother simply saw an old house and followed her nose to it – which is a way she has. I just don't have an idea of what you're talking about. But I suppose it must be whatever those crooks outside have come after. And we're going to stop them.'

'Then I'll tell you. It's the Christmas box.'

'The Christmas box? Isn't that a sort of present you give the letter-carrier and the ashman?'

Jay shakes his head. 'Not here. Our Christmas was a man.'

'Of course he was.' Grant has remembered. 'The sculptor who made the monument to Admiral Candleshoe in the chapel. And Mr Armigel said he made something for the house as well. Is that the box?'

'Yes – and you're going to see it – what can be seen of it, that is – now.' Jay turns and climbs again.

'And those fellows want to steal the box?'

'It's stranger than that.' Jay stops and opens a door. He continues to stand still for a moment, so that Lightning slips past and vanishes into darkness. 'You understand about the Long Gallery of a house like this? We're there now. But you must stay here at the door, please, until I get more light. The floor is bad.'

Grant, left waiting at the top of the stairway, finds that he is listening intently for sounds from the house below. It comes into his head that the enemy may have one of their number already concealed within, who is even now creeping to unbar some postern and admit his fellows. It would be possible, surely, for a patient ruffian to lurk undetected in a corner of Candleshoe for days – and may not such a one, therefore, have entered long before the present crisis aroused the extreme vigilance of the children? Or again, there are the two crazy old folk who are the house's only adult inhabitants. May one or the other not be tricked at any moment into answering a knock, a call? He realizes that these and a score of other questions which he himself is without the knowledge to formulate can never be out of Jay's head; they form the weight of public care that hangs on the boy's brow. Bows and arrows are very well – but Grant wishes he had a gun. Surely there must be at least a shot-gun, a sporting rifle, in the house? He remembers Mr Armigel's having said something about the last such weapon blowing to pieces in his hands.

Once more he listens intently – listens for a stealthy footstep on the dusty treads below him. There is no sound, and he crosses to the door of the Long Gallery and looks in. Jay is only half-way down, but in the murky perspective of the place he seems already a long way away. He is lighting a row of candles that stand in rusty sconces along the right-hand wall. Lightning stands beside him, his ears pricking into the darkness beyond. Jay turns and beckons. Grant takes another quick look behind him – he scarcely knows whether his behaviour is rational or panicky – and enters. Here and there the floor-boards have decayed and vanished. He treads carefully, and sees little of the gallery until he is standing beside the boy in the middle of it. Jay motions him to stand still, then moves on and lights more candles. As he nears the far end of the gallery something wholly bizarre becomes first faintly and then more clearly visible. It is as if the gallery were a tunnel ending in open air. Grant is looking into a little nocturnal glade between over-arching trees.

The thing gives him what the topiary garden gave : a brief moment of extreme strangeness. Then he sees that this is another ghost – the ghost of some departed modest revelry, a tattered remnant of stage *décor*. Perhaps it was Miss Candleshoe's brother Sir James who had a taste for private theatricals; perhaps it was Sir James's great-grandfather. But for its split second of illusion the thing has had Grant gaping – and this the boy has seen. Surprisingly, lithely, he vaults to the little stage and strikes an attitude; then his clear voice rings down the gallery :

> 'A fool, a fool! I met a fool i' the forest,
> A motley fool; a miserable world!
> As I do live by food, I met a fool . . .'

Jay's inky clothes are surely Hamlet's. But they do very well for Jaques – and for a moment the boy holds his pose before he jumps down from the stage. He is laughing at Grant. It is a queer carefree interlude, the appearance for a flash of a Jay troubled by no problems of generalship.

Then, grave again, he is pointing over Grant's shoulder. 'There!'

Grant turns round, making a quick survey of the whole place as he does so. It is panelled and has a plaster ceiling parts of which have come down; the height is inconsiderable, and except for two deep bays near either end the gallery cannot be more than six or seven yards broad. But it is at least fifty yards long, and the immense promenade which this permits of must have been the prime pride of Candleshoe once upon a time. The central floor-space is vacant – indeed little could now be set down there with safety – but along either wall there is an uninterrupted jumble of junk which makes the great hall downstairs appear a very orderly sight indeed. A few of the objects can be scarcely a century old: a weighing-machine, for instance, and a mechanical horse, and a variety of culinary and other domestic engines plainly of the Victorian age. But most of the stuff survives – after a fashion – from far earlier times, and some of it must represent the original furnishings of the gallery.

The two deep bays are in fact great windows, and opposite each is an elaborately carved fireplace. Or so Grant for a moment thinks. Then he sees that one of them (it is to this that Jay is pointing) is not a fireplace at all. It is Admiral Candleshoe's monument, done all over again. Grant positively rubs his eyes. He then sees that, this time, Gerard Christmas has done his work with a difference. It is the Admiral's monument once more – but this time the Admiral himself is missing. The flanking figures have lowered their curtains upon the watery scene. Between the spectator and the Admiral – if he is really there – are two massive slabs of marble, chiselled into heavy folds.

'There,' Jay repeats. 'That's the Christmas box. It has been called that always.'

Jay has slipped away to listen at the head of the staircase.

Grant is left staring. Lightning, aware that the monument – if it may be called that – is a focus of interest, goes up and sniffs at it. Perhaps for some sinister reason, perhaps merely because a cold draught from its crevices has tickled his nose, the hairs of his neck bristle. Jay returns and Grant speaks. 'I don't see any sense in it.' He is aware that this is a prosaic and inadequate reaction. But the thing can only be some sort of joke, and he is offended by the notion of a joke which must have entailed a great deal of human labour.

'That's because you don't know the story.' Jay takes Lightning by the collar and makes him lie down. 'Thomas Candleshoe was various things.'

'The Admiral?'

'He was that in the end. But he was only a captain when he sailed with Drake against the Armada. And although he was to inherit this house from his father, he was quite a poor man. Then he disappeared.'

'Disappeared? But didn't he go on something called the Islands Voyage?'

'That was nearly ten years later, and he was drowned on it. But what do you think he did in between?'

'Turned pirate, perhaps.'

Grant has spoken idly, saying merely what appears to be the appropriate thing. But Jay looks at him with swift distrust. 'So you *do* know something?'

'Nothing of the kind, Jay. I'm just taking a guess.'

'Well, he did. But it isn't really known. It's in an old book in the library – one that was printed just for members of the family. The first page says "Privately Printed in 1823".'

'It tells about Admiral Thomas having been a pirate?'

'Yes – and the legend of the Christmas box.'

'I see.' Grant looks at the heavy marble affair before which they are still standing. 'Do you know what a legend is?'

'Of course.' Jay's pale cheeks flush faintly. It is plain that he would quickly resent any rash reference to his circumscribed education. 'But a good many legends are – are founded in fact.'

'Is there treasure in this legend?'

'Yes.'

'And the treasure was hidden in the Christmas box – perhaps is there still?'

'Yes.' Jay is very pale again. Here is the core of some immense fantasy within which he lives. He fears incredulity far more than he fears the men now prowling outside Candleshoe.

'Wasn't the Admiral drowned before this house was built?'

'Two or three years before that.'

'Then he couldn't have done any hiding of treasure here himself?'

'Of course not – any more than he could have ordered his own monument, either in the chapel or here. Thomas's younger brother Robert, who was his heir, built this house – and paid for it perhaps with money from Thomas's treasure. He sold jewels and plate and coins that Thomas had won from the Spaniards, and gave the money to the masons and carpenters.'

Grant nods acceptively. 'That sounds likely enough, Jay. I'd say a good many English houses were paid for that way in the days of Drake. But when Robert had Gerard Christmas carve a monument to Admiral Thomas in the chapel, why did he get him to make this affair as well?'

'That's just the point!' Jay is eager. 'There was treasure that couldn't be sold – that couldn't be owned to. Don't you see? Thomas had been reckless about whom he robbed at sea. He had been a real pirate – not just a privateer pillaging only the Queen's enemies. So there was a great deal of wealth that couldn't possibly be owned to – not perhaps for hundreds of years. And that's why Robert Candleshoe had Christmas build him this secret chamber. It was to house the treasure in until later members of the family could safely use it.'

Jay is urgent, but at the same time he is perfectly matter-of-fact. Grant feels that he himself may presently be persuaded into actually accepting the boy's tall story. He looks again at the enigmatic structure before him, and it strikes him as being rather like a poem of the same tortuously-minded age: an elaborate conceit, and a chilly one. 'Don't you think', he asks, 'that it's rather an odd way of concealing treasure? A secure hiding place, surely, ought to be unnoticeable. This affair sets one a great puzzle at once.'

'Their minds didn't work like that.' Jay gives himself courteously to explanation. 'The story is that Robert and the Admiral's widow – Thomas was married, although he had no children – quarrelled over the form the monument should take. The widow had her way in the chapel, and Robert said the design was extravagant; was what we should call theatrical, or in bad taste. So Robert had this one, which he called chaster, set up here in the gallery of his new house. But all this story of a quarrel was, of course, only a blind. It covered the making of a small secret chamber by Christmas and his men. Christmas was very reliable. He had carved the figurehead of Admiral Candleshoe's ship, and he was in the family secret.'

'As you and I are now – not to mention those fellows out in the garden?' Jay's story hangs together after a fantastic fashion – but it is surely a yarn very much out of a boys' magazine. 'You say you read all this in a book printed more than a hundred years ago? If it was known like that, and there was really supposed to be treasure, surely one Candleshoe or another would have looked into it?'

'Looked into Christmas's box? But you can't. The entrance is a lost secret.'

Grant chuckles. 'It always is – in tales like this, Jay. But plenty of Candleshoes would have broken in with a crowbar, surely, if they'd believed there was wealth behind these hunks of marble.'

'They just didn't – and for two reasons.' Jay is now confident again in his story; his high state of tension has eased a little as he absorbs himself in retailing it; his right hand caresses Lightning, who has laid his nose between his paws and appears to be asleep. 'It did come, you see, to be thought of as only a legend. That was in the eighteenth century, which was a very – a very rational time.' This time, Jay smiles at his own ignorance. 'Is that the right word?'

'I think it is. And the other reason?'

'When people do become that – rational, I mean, and scorning old stories – they become secretly superstitious as well. And there is a superstition about the Christmas box which none of the Candleshoes has cared to go against. This too is in the old book. And it is this: that when the family's danger is greater than it has ever been, the Christmas box will open and – and save the situation. That part is silly, perhaps. But I like it, all the same.' Jay's eye is kindling again. 'Don't you?'

'I don't like the notion that there are a lot of crooks hanging around this place, thinking they will do themselves a whole heap of good by smashing up this gallery in a hunt for treasure from the Spanish Main. If they've got hold of the old story, it seems a pity.'

Grant speaks mildly. But he is startled to see the ironic twist that must be given to his own first near-shot at the actual state of affairs. He had thought of the crooks as after real booty – and at a sort of cross-purposes with the children, who are interpreting the situation in terms of their own private imaginings. But now it appears that the crooks are pursuing and the children defending the same fairy gold. It is wildly improbable that there is any truth in Jay's history or legend. Far more likely, although the boy does not realize it, is the story of the dispute over alternative monuments. Crooks however may well be persons of indifferent education, incapable of weighing evidence in a matter of this sort. Somehow they have got hold of Jay's story, and it has not occurred to them to disbelieve it.

'They must have got hold of the book, you see.' Jay continues patiently to explain. 'It was a great mistake to put such a thing in a book – even if it was to be, as they call it, privately printed. Wicked people were sure to get hold of a copy one day.'

'That may be true.' Grant looks again at the Christmas box, and a fresh consideration strikes him. 'Jay – have you measured? Is there more space to account for behind this monument than would be occupied by the old chimney-shaft?'

Jay nods; his anxiety to convince keeps him patient still. 'Yes, indeed. It would be difficult to show you in the dark, and you have to make measurements if you are really going to be sure. But I've worked it out that there is space for a room fifteen feet one way and eight feet the other. Robert Candleshoe could have got quite a lot of treasure into that.'

'Quite enough to set the place on its feet again.' Grant finds that, however heated he must suppose Jay's imagination to be, he has no disposition to distrust the boy's measurements. 'But why have you kept quiet about all this? Why are you chancing it that you and your friends will be able to beat this enemy alone? I'd say it would have been better to tell Miss Candleshoe and Mr Armigel. Or do you think them too cra – ' Grant checks himself. 'Do you think them too old to be reliable?'

There is a moment's silence. Jay is having one of his rare hesitations. He tugs at Lightning's ear, and the hound's tail, stirring in acknowledgement, sends up a little eddy of dust from the floor. 'Shall I tell you? I'm trusting you very far.'

'Sure. But you can go on trusting me, Jay.'

'Well, you see it's like this. When I was quite small, I used to imagine things.'

'I see.' Grant looks warily at the boy. 'And you grew out of it?'

'Of course. But at that time both Miss Candleshoe and Mr Armigel, who were more – more observant then, thought that I imagined things too much. They are very kind. But of course it is a long time – a very long time – since they were young like you and me.'

'It certainly is.' Grant feels unreasonably flattered.

'And then – when, as I say, I was much younger still, and really *quite* small – they were worried about this. They used to say that being alone here was bad, and that I ought to be sent away. I discovered, by listening when I shouldn't' – Jay flushes faintly – 'that Miss Candleshoe was inquiring about boarding-schools.'

'That was pretty handsome of her, wasn't it?'

Jay's flush deepens. 'You mean because I am only an orphan whose mother was – was an employee here? Yes, of course. But my mother died in an accident, you know, almost before I can remember her; and Miss Candleshoe has considered me a responsibility.' Jay articulates this last word very precisely. 'She is, I say, very kind. And because she has very little money now, I believe she would have sold something valuable here – we have still, you know, a few such things – to send me to this school. So at once I had to become different.'

'Different, Jay?'

'Not imagining things. I had to become a – a practical boy, who knew what could still be done with animals, and in the garden, and so that we can all continue to live here although there is less and less money. Have you asked Mr Armigel about me?'

Grant finds this direct challenge embarrassing. 'Mr Armigel has spoken of you.'

'Then he has certainly told you that I am not a boy who imagines things. Has he not?'

Grant grins. 'Sure.'

'It is a thing that pleases him, and Miss Candleshoe too. They feel that they have handled me well. But if I now told them the truth about this plot against the treasure in the Christmas box – '

'They would pack you off to that school after all?'

'There would be a danger of it, I think. Of course, they are both very old now, and you can't tell any longer how they will take things. That is why I have been anxious too about your mother. They might sell her Candleshoe, quite suddenly, in order to follow out some foolish plan of their own.'

'I believe they might.' Grant considers the boy soberly. 'See here, Jay – you are American born, just as I am. But I take it that your future is going to be here in England. And you know the English reckon it an advantage for a kid to have been at the kind of school Miss Candleshoe was probably thinking of?'

'I'm not interested in that.' This time Jay's reply is like a flash.

'Do you know what would happen if my mother did buy Candleshoe?'

'Builders and decorators and insolent servants from London.'

'Maybe so.' Grant reflects that a streak of something very lordly is evident at times in Jay's speech. 'But she'd consider herself as taking over the livestock too.'

'The livestock?' Jay glances at Lightning – and then back at Grant as comprehension comes to him. 'You mean me?'

'Just that. And if you weren't a polite kind of boy your reply would be "Damn her impudence" – wouldn't it?

But she would think the world of you as her very own discovery, and probably want to send you to an even grander –'

'I prefer, please, to be nobody's discovery but my own.' Jay looks at Grant with a directness that shows him to attach a clear significance to this statement. Then he seems to feel that some softening civility should be added. 'Your mother is a tremendously wealthy person?'

'Wealthier, I'd say, than Lord Scattergood and half the other marquesses of England rolled up together.'

'That must be very nice.'

Grant laughs aloud. 'You mean, don't you, "My God, how awful"? They do seem, Jay, to have made an utter Englishman of you.'

Jay frowns. 'All that – about England and America, I mean – is something that I must think about at another time.'

'Quite right, son. Just at this moment, you do seem to have quite enough on your plate already. But listen. There really are crooks hanging about Candleshoe. They've wrecked my car. And I've seen one of them myself, sending signals to others. If we bring in the police and clear them up, nobody can possibly say you've been imagining things.'

'There would be a – an inquiry into the Christmas box. It might be opened. The treasure might be taken by – by the Government, by the Queen. Doesn't that happen to treasure trove?'

'I don't know what the law would say about it, Jay. But suppose there really is a treasure. Mightn't it be of more use to the Government, or to the Queen, than just lying behind all that marble? And it wouldn't be of much significance to any one so very old as Miss Candleshoe, would it? And there don't seem to be any other Candleshoes within sight. The family looks like being extinct, and the old Admiral's hoard still untouched.'

'I have thought about all that.' Jay is cautious again. 'But I see it differently, somehow. I think I believe in the legend, in a way. That there will be a crisis, I mean, and that Candleshoe will be saved by the secret of the Christmas box being revealed at that moment.'

'Isn't that what's called imagining things?'

Jay opened his eyes wide. 'I didn't say I *had* stopped imagining things. I'd as soon stop living. Wouldn't you?'

# CHAPTER THIRTEEN

GRANT FEATHER, who is going to be a great writer and transform what he likes to call 'the creative situation' on the North American continent, feels rather shattered by this *coup* on the part of the son of Candleshoe's deceased housekeeper. He takes another look round the Long Gallery and is constrained to admit that a boy who, having the run of such a place, yet refused to give his fancy some rein in it would be sadly wasting his opportunities. Not Jaques alone haunts the cobweb and tattered canvas of that derelict stage; Rosalind and Celia too lurk in the wings – and Touchstone, and the lioness, and the green and gilded snake. They have been there a full two years, likely enough – ever since Robin Hood and Friar Tuck made way for them. And here, behind the boldly incised marble of Gerard Christmas, lies half the treasure of the Spanish Main. Had Admiral Candleshoe one leg or two? Impossible to tell, since even that other and more informative monument submerges him up to the neck in his petrified ocean. But it is a good guess that in Jay's mind he is still not wholly distinct from Long John Silver, and that this mouldering gallery has often been the deserted deck of the *Hispaniola*, with Israel Hands lying in a pool of blood in the scuppers. It has been too the Admiral Benbow tavern near midnight, with Jim Hawkins bending over the dead mariner, and hearing suddenly upon the frozen road –

Grant gives a jump that brings Lightning to his feet, his spine once more bristling. From somewhere beyond the confines of the dimly-lit gallery comes a faint but crisp tap-tap. For a moment the sound seems to penetrate from beyond the enigmatical marble curtains before which Grant and Jay stand – and for a moment too it suggests overpoweringly a stick in the hands of a blind man. Then there is a murmur of voices and the illusion dissipates itself. Miss Candleshoe has entered the gallery. Old ladies, as well as blind pirates, get about with the aid of a stick.

Miss Candleshoe taps her way forward with a very reasonable caution, holding up a lantern in her free hand. Behind her come Mrs Feather and Mr Armigel, amiably conversing. It is apparent that the chatelaine of Candleshoe is courteously affording her guest a view of the principal antiquities of the house. Grant sees that the process of secular and undisturbed decay everywhere revealed has gone to his mother's head. Candleshoe in its more than centennial trance is her own absolute discovery; destiny has led her to this spot as designedly as it ever led Aeneas to the Lavinian shore; so urgently is her cheque-book occupied in burning a hole in her handbag that Grant can almost see the incandescence in what is still the half-darkness of the gallery.

Miss Candleshoe comes to a halt, raises the lantern above her head, and nods approvingly. 'So Jay has already thought to show your grandson round. That was most sensible. He has always been a sensible lad. And I see that he is drawing attention to the Christmas box, upon which Mr Armigel has lately been informing you.'

'Now, isn't that just thrilling?' Mrs Feather advances in a condition of happy awe that makes her son grind his teeth. 'To think, Grant, that this gallery has one of the finest priest's holes in the country!'

'Is *that* what the Christmas box is?' Grant, as he turns to Mr Armigel, glimpses a flicker of resigned disgust on Jay's face.

'Most certainly, my dear sir – most certainly it is. There have, of course, been other stories. But, although entertaining, they must be dismissed as fanciful. A priest's hole it most assuredly is.'

Grant is conscious that at Candleshoe at the moment

there are matters of more urgent consideration than the probable purpose of Gerard Christmas's obscure fabrication. Nevertheless Mr Armigel's proposition raises a problem of historical scholarship which a university student ought not to let pass. 'Do you mean', he asks, 'that at one time the Candleshoes were Catholics?'

'Catholics?' Mr Armigel is momentarily perplexed. 'Ah – *Roman* Catholics. But most assuredly not. The family, I am glad to say, has never since the Reformation felt any attraction to the errors of Rome.'

'In that case would they *want* a priest's hole?'

But at this Miss Candleshoe herself chimes in with some spirit. 'And pray, sir, why should they *not* want a priest's hole? It would appear to me to be a most reasonable form of accommodation in any gentleman's mansion. Indeed, I can recall our late Vicar remarking to my brother Sir James that, in the vicarage, such an apartment would be invaluable to him.'

'Precisely so.' Mr Armigel takes off his glasses and placidly polishes them. 'I am disposed to believe, moreover, that Robert Candleshoe, in adding this amenity to his new residence, was actuated by a humanitarian feeling all too rare at that time. In a high-spirited household, we must recall, the life of a domestic chaplain was at times subject to extraordinary casualties. Particularly on days when there was no hunting.'

Grant is bewildered. 'You mean they hunted the chaplain?'

'Exactly. It was harmless, of course, but harassing. Now William Shakespeare – you know William Shakespeare?'

'Sure.'

'I am very glad to hear it. He appears to me the very greatest writer of the late age. Well, in his tragedy of *Hamlet*, Shakespeare has a reference, I believe, to this simple old English sport. The young hero, about to elude his wicked uncle's guards, cries out "Hide fox and all after". The allusion is undoubtedly to the robust old sport of Hunt the Chaplain. But Robert Candleshoe, not wishing future chaplains here to be subjected to this good-humoured but exhausting exigency, caused Christmas to build by way of an earth, you might say – the concealed chamber which is the subject of our present discussion.'

Grant, as he listens to this, catches another glimpse of Jay. The boy is immobile, and in an attitude of strained listening. And Grant sees that it is time he himself weighed in. In point of imagining things it is these two ancient persons who really make all the going; and it is Jay who is in contact with hard, if enigmatical, fact. Grant decides that the situation decidedly requires opening up. 'But there are stories', he asks Mr Armigel, 'that the Christmas box was used for concealing valuable property?'

'Certainly. But I much doubt whether there could ever have been any foundation for rumours of that kind.'

'Still, the place could have been used for that – and could still be used for it now?'

'My dear sir, the secret of ingress to our priest's hole has been lost, time out of mind.'

'But it could be found again?'

Mr Armigel is a shade perplexed by this insistence. 'I judge it probable that there was a mechanism of some little complexity, which by this time will assuredly have ceased to operate. To penetrate to the chamber now, a gang of stonemasons would be required. And family sentiment has been, on the whole, adverse to the idea of investigation.'

'But repairs could doubtless be effected.' Miss Candleshoe makes this point with some emphasis. 'No doubt the mechanism of which Mr Armigel speaks could be located and put in very good order. And I have no doubt that a thoroughly convenient priest's hole would result.'

'Certainly.' Mr Armigel backs up his patroness. 'And the situation being dry and airy, it could scarcely fail of being salubrious. But unfortunately we are not in a position to investigate further this evening.'

'That's just too bad.' Grant shakes his head. 'For a really burglar-proof strong-room is just what Candleshoe needs right now.'

It is Mrs Feather who sees that Grant offers this odd remark with some serious purpose. 'Candleshoe needs a strong-room! Now, just what would that mean?'

'I'll explain.' Grant turns to Miss Candleshoe. 'I don't want to alarm you, marm, more than need be. But the fact is that a gang of crooks – '

'I beg your pardon?' Miss Candleshoe is wholly at sea.

'The fact is that a band of robbers is prowling about outside this house now. I believe they are determined to break in. And as they must expect to get away with objects of very considerable value, I say it's a pity you can't tuck away whatever these may be in the Christmas box.'

'Robbers? Objects of very considerable value?' For the moment, both these conceptions appear to perplex Miss Candleshoe equally.

'I'm perfectly serious.' Grant turns to Mr Armigel. 'Jay knows about this too. And Jay, I can see, is a very sensible boy, with a strong practical turn of mind.'

'Very true.' Mr Armigel nods with vigour. 'Jay, I think I may venture to declare, has turned out a lad with both his feet planted firmly on earth. But surely, my dear sir – '

'Well, Jay has taken some useful measures about this threat, but it remains a very urgent one.'

'The men-servants must be armed.' Miss Candleshoe, rising to the occasion, speaks with feudal resolution. 'And a mounted groom must be dispatched for the soldiery. It is at moments like these that I particularly regret the death of my dear brother Sir James. In addition to being a first-class shot he had a notable skill with man-traps. Mr Armigel, be so kind as to ring the bell.'

But this time the chaplain appears to be in no mood for empty ritual. He addresses Grant. 'When I come to think of it, I have been aware of suspicious characters about the place for some little time. Only the day before yesterday a totally strange person penetrated to the great hall on the pretext of wishing to read what he called, I think, the gas meter. It was most perplexing. Of course I called in Jay, who at once persuaded the fellow to leave. But how these marauders could – um – come to suppose that we cherish at Candleshoe any objects of large pecuniary value is wholly baffling to me. We still own, it is true, a little family plate. But the *res angusta domi* must be only too evident among us.'

'Then there is nothing of really great value?' Grant is briskly challenging.

Mr Armigel removes his spectacles for the purpose of giving a brisk rub to his nose; and when he answers, it is with a question of his own. 'Might these villains be thinking of the Christmas box? Might they have heard the legends of treasure, and so forth?'

'I suppose they might. Jay here – who has thought this out in a very cool, clear-headed way –'

Mr Armigel manages to return the spectacles to his nose without interrupting a vigorous nod. 'I have no doubt that Jay takes a sound practical view of the matter.'

'Jay is inclined to suppose that it is the Christmas box they are after. But, if there is anything else, I think we ought to have – well, complete frankness, Mr Armigel. If there is something else that needs hiding away, let us get on with the job while we can.'

'A most prudent suggestion. But, if I may say so, all the Candleshoe skeletons are securely in their cupboards already.' Mr Armigel allows himself a pardonable chuckle at this mild witticism, and in this Miss Candleshoe herself somewhat unexpectedly joins. 'Do I understand you to suppose that these villains are actually on the point of endeavouring to break in?'

'Yes, sir. I've seen two of them in the gardens myself. And, what's more, they've wrecked our automobile.'

'Wrecked our automobile?' Mrs Feather looks incredulously at her son.

'Yes, momma. The automobile won't stir again without a new magneto. These people are just taking no chances, and they have Candleshoe very nicely isolated for the night.'

'I just can't believe it.' Most unwontedly, Mrs Feather for a moment allows mere bewilderment to overwhelm her. 'A sweet, peaceful spot like this! Why, out in the garden, in that romantic moonlight, I was feeling –'

'Out in the garden?' Jay, who has been silent since his elders entered the gallery, snaps out this question. Everybody is startled. He takes a stride forward. 'You have been outside since I saw you last?'

'Certainly I have – right now. When Mr Armigel was showing me the library I remembered there was moonlight, and I wanted badly to see the effect of it on this beautiful building. So I just slipped out –'

'You mean you unbolted a shutter and went out on the terrace?'

'Yes, Jay. Mr Armigel was kind enough to help me to –'

'Fools!' The words leap from the lips of a Jay blazing with anger. 'When you came back – did it occur to you to bolt it again?'

'I don't think –'

But Mrs Feather's reply is lost in a commotion that tells its own story. From somewhere far below them comes a crash and a shout. There is a moment's silence and then a second crash, a hubbub of children's voices, and what can only be a scream of pain. Jay is off down the gallery like a flash. He shouts over his shoulder to Grant, and Grant follows. As they reach the head of the staircase by which they had climbed to the Long Gallery the turmoil below becomes momentarily louder. Then it is swamped by the clangour of that alarm bell which Grant has already heard once tonight. This time he can feel the floor tremble beneath him as it peals.

# CHAPTER FOURTEEN

Jay's mode of getting downstairs in a hurry is simple. He leaps clean from one turn to the next, and as he does so contrives a right-angled twist in air; as he lands he is thus in position for his next leap. Miraculously, his lantern remains alight, but the trajectory thus enforced upon it nullifies its function as an illuminant. To Grant the treads beneath his feet become no more than a meaningless dance of shadows; he judges it best simply to jump when Jay jumps; and this he manages successfully enough till the last flight of all, when he stumbles and arrives in the lobby head over heels and with the breath knocked out of him. Jay goes straight on unheeding. For a second or two Grant gropes about in darkness, and then manages to stagger into the hall.

Here the lamps are still burning, and he sees at the farther end the uncleared table, with half-a-dozen baked apples still on their dish. He puts on a sprint to overtake Jay, but his eye travels round the place once more as he runs, and it comes to him powerfully that this whole adventure is nonsense. The solid and unremarkable Jacobean furniture; the moth-eaten trophies of the chase that jostle with the darkened and indecipherable canvases on the walls; the cupboards and chests overflowing with the rubbish of centuries; the armour, now lying about in disregarded heaps, which innocently pretentious Candleshoes must have bought cheap on the antique market centuries ago: there is surely absolutely nothing in all this that could excite the cupidity of a sneak-thief, let alone an unascertained number of formidable ruffians.

Grant swears, and quickens his pace further. From in front of him he hears sounds that make him wish

Candleshoe and all its mouldering junk at the bottom of the sea. Whether or not the presence of these criminals is senseless, they are indisputably within the walls of Candleshoe – and, equally indisputably, Jay's forces are waging a pitched battle with them at this moment. Some of the children – Grant has marked – are far younger even than Jay. This is shocking in itself – but even more alarming is the fact that the elder children, at least, have weapons which, if they can be brought favourably into play, are likely to be quite as accurate as any gangster's gun. Such power, if used, invites reprisals by unscrupulous men secure of themselves in this empty countryside.

Grant jumps to the dais, vaults the table, and is out of the hall. On his right, he remembers, is Miss Candleshoe's drawing-room. But the uproar comes from the end of a corridor on his left, and he realizes that here the house ramifies beyond its original plan. Some flicker of prosperity after Robert Candleshoe's time must have enabled one of his descendants to add thus to the consequence of the mansion. Grant races forward, turns a corner, tumbles through an open door, and is straightway in the midst of pandemonium.

It is certainly a library, and a surprisingly extensive one; there is quite enough light to see that. The light however has a flickering or flame-like quality most appropriately suggestive of an infernal region; there would be nothing out of the way in the momentary appearance amid it of a pitchfork, a cloven hoof, or a forked tail; and this expectation is powerfully reinforced by the yelling and screaming which fill the dust-laden air. For a moment the confusion seems hopeless. Grant takes a grip on himself and realizes that he must master its elements one at a time. Then he can act, if any effective action is possible.

The light comes from nearly a dozen small electric torches, jettisoned by the children in the course of the current mêlée, and now being rolled and kicked about the floor as an unnoticed by-product of the same titanic struggle. They add to the insecurity of anyone who manages to get momentarily to his feet; and so too does the circumstance that the terrain is littered with books that have been swept from their shelves in some earlier phase of the conflict.

In the wall facing Grant are three tall windows. Those on either flank are shuttered and bolted; the shutters of the middle aperture are drawn back, and what appears to be a french window beyond them has been wrenched open; it is here, Grant realizes, that his mother has so fatally tampered with the efficiency of Jay's defences. But the force which has entered as yet through this breach seems to be restricted to a single individual now momentarily submerged beneath an ominously heaving heap of children. Grant sees that it would be a good idea to get the fatal shutters firmly closed again. He has little doubt that the enemy can muster a considerably larger power than this.

And then Grant sees that what is going on is in fact a struggle for the open window. The library has a system of bays constituting a bottle-neck which the struggling children are trying to force; their enemy is endeavouring to hold them at bay in order to cover the species of beach-head behind him. But why has he not been supported through this established breach already? As Grant asks himself this he sees a wavering light in the outer darkness framed by the open window – and a moment later he hears, from somewhere close above his head, a *twang* already familiar to him at Candleshoe, and this is immediately followed by a warning shout from outside. Grant turns and glances upwards. Uncertainly behind a cloud of dust which is almost as thick as a curtain he can just distinguish the boy Robin, perched on the cornice of a massive bookcase, steadying himself against some bust of the classical variety conventionally proper in such places, and with his bow still quivering in his outstretched hand. While the main body of Jay's supporters has been fighting its way towards the window, Robin has been covering it from this point of vantage. Grant, remembering that the invasion of the library has been a wholly unexpected turn in the siege, has to admit that the deployment of the defenders has been a triumph of general preparedness.

'Last arrow fired. Two men coming.' It is Robin's voice from above; he speaks loudly and rapidly, but nevertheless with the impassivity of a player making some necessary announcement in the course of a game. Grant sees that it is the moment of crisis, squares his shoulders, and prepares to charge. There is just a chance that he can burst through the scrum and make fast those shutters in time.

'Stop!' It is Jay who is beside him. The boy has tugged a tall library ladder from the wall, and now thrusts it into Grant's hands. 'Hold on till I say "Shove". And then send it straight over them.'

'Sure.' Grant feels that he can be as reliable a lieutenant as Robin at a pinch. He holds the ladder pointing at the ceiling; Jay swarms up it like a circus child doing some perfectly familiar turn, and at a word Grant gives a shove; with gathering velocity Jay describes a curve in air, and lands like a cat by the window while the ladder comes down with a nasty thud on the backs of the milling supporters now behind him. As a commander Jay has his decidedly ruthless moments. But he has slammed to the shutters and bolted them just as a heavy body crashes against them from the outside.

It looks like victory. Somebody, seeing this, gives a shout of triumph. The effect is unfortunate; it distracts the children and fires their isolated and virtually captive enemy to a last effort. The man staggers to his knees and then to his feet. He kicks out viciously and then, still clutched by tenacious hands, hurls his full weight against the nearest library bay. From the lower shelves of this the books have already been swept, and it is top-heavy; it tilts and a further half-dozen tiers of massive volumes come showering to the floor; it tilts further and falls with a crash, the force of which is fortunately in part taken by the mass of material it has just discharged. Dust for a full half-minute reduces visibility to nil, and nobody in the library has power to do anything but choke and gasp.

As the air begins to clear it becomes evident that the situation has sharply deteriorated. The invader is behind the barrier of the fallen bookcase. In one hand he has a torch with which he is exploring the disposition of the defenders. In the other hand he has a revolver. Grant looks hard at this and cannot persuade himself that the thing is a toy or a fake. Even so, it may not be loaded. And, even if indeed loaded, the probability is that the fellow has very little disposition to murder. He may be prepared to use the weapon if it is a question of avoiding capture; he may be unprepared to use it in the face of mere passive resistance and an injunction to clear out. Grant tries to apply these considerations to the single problem before him: the safety of this crowd of excited children. And for the same purpose he tries to size up the man. He has not the appearance of a successful gangster. Even before this rough-house began he must have cut a shabby figure, and now he looks as if he had been tipped out of an ash-cart. Partly because he has had most of the breath knocked out of him, and partly – Grant guesses – because he is scared stiff, the gun and the torch both tremble in his hands. But, if the gun is really loaded, there is very little comfort in the supposition that he may be terrified and barely in control of himself.

The children stand immobile, fascinated. The man's glance travels over them and pauses on Jay. He licks his lips and speaks in a voice that betrays the same tremor as his hands. 'Open those shutters.' Nobody stirs. He swings his gun round until it is levelled at the boy. 'Open them – quick!'

'You are our prisoner. Put that thing down.' Jay speaks and makes no move.

'Open those shutters, or I fire.'

'Put it down, or I shall come for it.'

The air is clearer now. Grant can see enough of the man's face to dislike it. He dislikes a twitch at the mouth. He decides that there is just enough take-off to give him an outside chance of clearing the bookcase at a straight-on jump. He decides too that the thing must be fought out at whatever risk to the defenders – this simply because Jay has no thought of anything else.

'I'm coming now.' Jay looks straight at the man and walks deliberately forward. From his standing start Grant hurls himself into the three paces he can afford before taking off. At the same moment some sort of thunderbolt crashes down on the man with the gun and sends him sprawling. It is Robin who has launched himself from his bookcase. He has been the forgotten factor in the affair.

Jay is sitting on the floor, and Grant guesses that he is wondering if he is going to be ingloriously sick. Courage must sometimes be paid for in humiliating ways. Robin, who ought to have broken both his legs, is only badly winded; even so, he manages to gasp out orders that have the effect of covering his leader's temporary withdrawal from the direction of affairs. Robin must be one of the supreme lieutenants of all time. And both these boys must own a demon. Nothing else can account for the morale of the small and absurdly juvenile force at their disposal. The children are now dispersing to their former action-stations with the phlegm of a crack division deploying under fire.

Grant takes a look at the vanquished enemy. He lies motionless on his back – horrifyingly helpless and deflated and dirty. His complexion is as grey as the dust that coats it and there is blood coming from his nose and mouth. Jay gets rather shakily to his feet and joins Grant. 'Do you think', he asks carefully, 'that this man is dead?'

'He's some way from that. But he'll be senseless for quite some time. And something rather nasty may have happened to his skull.'

'Ought we to shove him out, so that they can get him to a doctor? There's Robin's father.'

'I don't know that they would think their casualty all that important, Jay. And the right person to get to Robin's father is Robin.'

Jay swings round. 'Robin isn't hurt?'

'Strangely enough he doesn't seem to be. But I don't mean that. I mean that somebody – somebody who knows the ground, I'm afraid – must get out of this and through to your nearest village. If that's where Robin lives, let Robin make for home, and get his father to call out all the police he can. You see, this must stop.'

'I don't know that I do see.'

'Be honest with yourself, Jay, and you will. This is a siege. It's our business to hold out. But we must also plan to be relieved as soon as may be. That's just plain sense.'

Jay nods. His decisions are always rapid. 'Very well. Robin, will you go?'

'Of course I'll go if you ask me to.' Robin, who has got his wind back, is as matter-of-fact as ever. 'It's just a matter of getting clear.'

'I think I can fix that. It's a diversion that's required, and that will be my part of the affair.' As he speaks, Grant stoops and picks up the unconscious man's revolver. He knows in an instant that it is unloaded. The crooks, as he had half-guessed, have not trusted so jittery a member of their body with the live thing. He slips the weapon casually into his pocket. 'Yes – I can do quite a lot in the way of a diversion, I reckon. Particularly now that I've gotten a gun.'

# CHAPTER FIFTEEN

LORD ARTHUR SPENDLOVE, although a well-built man in good condition, had some difficulty in heaving that distinguished Roman connoisseur, Dr Rosenwald, into the ancient, powerful, and capacious car that he had chosen for the purpose of the expedition to Candleshoe. Even when this had been managed there was some further delay, since Mr Archdeacon had vanished in search of what he called – somewhat enigmatically – the relevant documents. Lord Scattergood, still not altogether convinced that firearms might not come in handy if a working hypothesis was sighted, muttered gloomily that his somnolent guest stank like a taproom. Brown, who alone bore the responsibility of seeing the party off, seemed to be of a similar mind, since every now and then he took a short walk into middle distance as if in quest of purer air. When Mr Archdeacon at length appeared, Brown bade him an affectionate farewell and at once withdrew into the house. It would have been possible to feel that, in Brown's view, a certain lack of aristocratic poise marked this nocturnal hue and cry after a couple of missing canvasses.

The moon, now riding high in a clear sky, gave to Benison itself and all its policies something the air of a vast canvas, cycloramically disposed. The main façade, with its long march of Ionic columns diminishing in either direction into distance and its broad flights of shallow steps descending from terrace to terrace amid an ordered profusion of sentries – Amazonian for the most part – in marble and bronze, seemed at once as insubstantial and as prodigal as an illusion conjured up out of paint-pots of the largest size. When Arthur let in his clutch and the car moved forward, it might have been this whole inordinate ostentation that was trundling by on rollers, after the fashion of that gorgeous species of visual entertainment which has been so unhappily superseded by the cinema. The West Pavilion, the Orangery, the Water Steps, the Temple of Ancient Virtue, the Neptune Fountain: all these flowed successively past – and each with the air of claiming that burst of applause reserved by the informed audience for some undoubted *chef d'œuvre* of the scene-painter's art. And on all this theatrical traffic the moon, like limelight expertly manipulated from somewhere up in the gallery, shed a soft radiance exactly tinted to make the very most of the bravura nature of the spectacle.

The car had gained the park, and was running past the sixth marquess's improved milking-parlour in the Chinese taste, before anybody spoke. Then Arthur addressed Mr Archdeacon, who was sitting beside him. 'I think you would say we want to mind what we're about?'

'Most decidedly. You will recall that almost my first observation was to the effect that this matter stands in a posture of some delicacy. In this, reflection now confirms me.'

'If I remember anything of old Miss Candleshoe, she won't stand for very much.'

'Precisely. Indeed, my dear Lord Arthur, your remark can be described only as a meiosis. Miss Candleshoe is unlikely to stand for anything at all. Caution will be necessary in addressing her. I am disposed to wonder, however, whether we shall in fact be the first persons to approach her on the subject of the missing Titians.'

'What's that?' Lord Scattergood, who had resigned himself to making this perplexing journey by the side of the slumbering Rosenwald, thrust forward a head which – perhaps with some dim memory of what is appropriate in a person engaged upon detective investigation – he has encased in an ancient deerstalker hat. 'What is that, Archdeacon, about other people being after the Titians?'

'I have been visited by a disturbing memory. Or rather' – and Mr Archdeacon produced simultaneously his pipe and his best metaphysical manner – 'I have been visited by a memory, trivial in itself, which our present exigency renders susceptible of a disturbing, if not indeed of a positively sinister, interpretation. Do I make myself clear?'

'Something fishy – eh?' Long practice had enabled Lord Scattergood to keep up wonderfully with his learned librarian.

'Exactly. As you know, I am one of those who take parties round Benison on Wednesday and Saturday afternoons.'

'And very nice of you too, my dear fellow.' Lord Scattergood, although himself at present engaged in this monotonous occupation every day of the week, was clearly conscience-stricken that the family oracle should have to retrench his meditations in the same interest.

'Not at all. There is much food for thought in both the bearing and the conversation of our visitors. Volumes could be written upon them.'

'That's very true.' Lord Scattergood cheered up on being presented with this elevated view of the matter. 'And I hope you'll bring out something of the sort with a good publisher. Sermons in stones, and all that – what?'

'Approximately that, no doubt.' Mr Archdeacon, who had the kindliest feeling for the simplicity of his employer, benevolently puffed tobacco at him as if intent upon fumigating the deerstalker. 'But what I speak of is an incident perhaps three Wednesdays back. I had a small party, nearly every individual in which might without disparagement be described as a familiar type. One must remark, by the way, that the relationship between type and individual opens up a wide field of philosophic reference.'

'Yes, indeed.' It was Arthur who hastily interposed. 'But something happened, all the same?'

'In a modified sense of the term – yes.' This time Mr Archdeacon puffed at Arthur. 'There was an episode or incident. Or perhaps it would be more precise to say an occurrence.'

'I see.' Arthur found himself thrusting rather recklessly at the accelerator. 'But go on.'

'There were three men who – quite unwittingly – distinguished themselves from the group. Each preserved to the others the bearing of a stranger. Yet it was apparent to me that, in fact, some relationship existed between them. We come here upon the whole absorbing subject of intuitive perceptions. I myself incline to the interpretation of such phenomena in terms of simple hyperaesthesia.'

'Being on the *qui vive* – eh?' Once more Lord Scattergood had hit the nail remarkably straight on the head. 'And what did these fellows do then?'

'When we got to the octagon room, two of them simply fell to staring out of the window. This in itself, of course, was a circumstance by no means untoward. Many of our visitors are chiefly struck by the fact that the outer frames of the windows are protected by gold-leaf and not by paint. Others give their whole attention to scanning the gardens – presumably in order to determine if they are worth a further half-crown. But now comes the rub, my dear Marquess. The third man minutely scrutinized the Titians.'

'That's common enough, too.' Lord Scattergood had his own powers of observation and inference. 'There are people, you know, who understand no more about painting than I do, who believe that the impressive thing before a picture is to rub their noses on it, or peer in a ferocious way into the top left-hand corner. Just self-consciousness, I'd say, in simple folk feeling rather small in a big place. No vice in it – no vice in it at all. Prefer them to Rosenwald here, any day.'

Arthur Spendlove swung the car out into the high road. 'Do you mean that this chap had a go at the Titians in a professional-looking way? Not like the simple folk trying to impress themselves, but like our friend in the back seat making what he calls an expertise?'

'You describe it very well.' Mr Archdeacon could be dimly descried as nodding, Jove-like, within his cloud. 'But it is in the sequel that the chief significance of the incident resides. Having completed his inspection, this person made his way unobtrusively first to the one and then to the other of the remaining two men. To each he rapidly muttered something – and while still endeavouring to sustain the appearance of being a stranger. This interested me very much. I have remarked a similar convention of conduct in cinematographic entertainments dealing with low life and criminal practice.'

'Gangsters?' Lord Scattergood was much struck by this. 'Do you think these rascals came sneaking back, and somehow managed to steal the pictures? If so, aren't we on a fool's errand now? And in danger of being needlessly offensive to this poor old soul at Candleshoe?'

'I think not.' For a few moments Mr Archdeacon, who possessed a nice sense of climax, brooded in silence. 'For account must be taken of the reaction of the first man to his study of the paintings, and of the other men to the intelligence then covertly communicated to them. It was one of consternation.'

'Bless my soul! You think they had tumbled to what this Rosenwald person discovered tonight?'

'I judge that there can be no doubt of it. The man who scrutinized the supposed Titians was sufficiently expert in these matters to know that they were not what they were held out to be. I should add that he presently made to approach me.'

'What's that?' Arthur was really startled. 'He was going to tackle you about it?'

'The matter bore that appearance – or rather, I ought to say, does now so bear it. I simply had an impression – no more than a fleeting impression, upon which my mind did not again dwell until the revelation of this evening – that this man was minded to address himself to me; and that one of his companions – his clandestine companions, be it remembered – restrained him. I now pass to the succeeding Saturday.'

'You what?' Lord Scattergood had become a little dazed in the effort to follow all this.

'I have now to record a further incident, at the time apparently unrelated to the first, which an irresistibly logical compulsion now, however, obliges us to concatenate with it. As so often in the history of ratiocinative processes, the apparently casual reveals itself as being, in fact, within the sphere of the causal. This is something which you must frequently have remarked.'

Again Arthur made the car leap forward. 'Just what happened on the Saturday?'

'I can be very brief.' Mr Archdeacon paused – a sure sign that he was winding himself up for one of his most sustained rhetorical flights. Arthur again punched at the accelerator – and at this, whether by casual or causal impulsion, the oracle really did deliver himself with some conciseness. 'A lady of unexceptional conversation and address spent some time with me after my party had dispersed. I found her – um – singularly charming. She was most interested in what we had done with our more valuable things during the war. She asked me about the Old Masters in particular – remarking that her brother had stored a collection of some importance in a salt-mine in Wales. She had never heard of Candleshoe, but when I explained that our paintings had gone there, she appeared to be uncommonly curious about it, and asked a number of questions. You will agree that all this must now appear significant.'

'Uncommonly.' Lord Scattergood put unflawed intellectual conviction into this reply. 'But of what? Have you any ideas there, my dear fellow?'

'The indications all point to attempted theft. The three men were making a preliminary survey of the ground, preparatory to stealing the Benison Titians. And they were no common thieves, since they included among their number an expert capable of detecting what our pilgrim from Rome has detected. Moreover they were in a position to command the services of a woman of genteel bearing, who elicited from me that the genuine paintings had for some years been at Candleshoe Manor. To Candleshoe Manor we are now ourselves proceeding. In the popular old phrase, the plot thickens.'

Lord Scattergood considered this for some time. 'You think, Archdeacon, that these people may themselves have gone to Candleshoe and got a further line on the affair? They may have discovered who is likely to have abstracted our Titians from under the old lady's nose and left those shocking fakes instead?'

'I have no doubt whatever that they carried their inquiries to Candleshoe.'

Having said so much, the Marquess of Scattergood's sage withdrew upon that obscurity within which he delighted to enshroud himself. The tobacco-smoke became so thick in the car that Dr Rosenwald woke up coughing, offered some observations in a German surprisingly unrefined, and went to sleep again. There was a silence which was presently broken by Arthur, who addressed his father. 'What Archdeacon has in mind is this: that having learnt about Candleshoe and taken themselves off there, these rascals might find it unnecessary to take themselves further.'

'My dear boy, I don't at all understand you. If they were hot on the scent of our pictures – '

'The point is that the scent may have *ended* at Candleshoe.'

'Ended at Candleshoe?' The car travelled about a quarter of a mile while Lord Scattergood addressed his labouring mind to the implication of this. 'You can't mean – '

'It seems to be what Archdeacon means. I'm bound to say it wouldn't be the first thing to come into my own head.'

Abruptly Lord Scattergood lowered a couple of windows, and his librarian once more became visible. 'Archdeacon, my dear fellow, you can't mean this scandalous thing?' Lord Scattergood was much shocked. 'You don't suggest that this crazy but respectable old person – a kinswoman of mine, after a fashion, mark you – has stolen my Titians?'

For a moment Mr Archdeacon seemed unwilling to vouchsafe any reply to this plea; he puffed so hard that the air-stream now flowing through the car became a ribbon of smoke. Then, very slowly, he fetched from a capacious pocket a small portfolio of dark leather, secured with green tape. 'I have here', he presently pronounced, 'the relevant documentation of the affair.'

'You mean that you've been having inquiries made – that sort of thing?' Lord Scattergood was aghast.

'My inquiries, my dear Marquess, have been confined within the limits of the seventeenth and eighteenth centuries. Lord Arthur, pray stop the conveyance.'

'Draw up?' Arthur took his foot from the accelerator and looked in some surprise at his father's librarian.

'Precisely. Before we reach Candleshoe, it is highly desirable that you should be apprised – or is it reminded? – of certain historical circumstances connected with the family. Their almost alarmingly apposite nature has only come to me, I confess, as a result of the revelations of the present evening. Had they been within my knowledge on an anterior occasion, I might well have hesitated to embark with Candleshoe on the relations that I did. Regrets, however, are vain. I now propose to read to you – Marquess, will you switch on that light? – from the private diaries of William Spendlove, the first earl. I make bold to say that an acquaintance with what he has to say will be of some guidance to you later tonight. Shall I begin?'

'Certainly, my dear Archdeacon. We are entirely in your hands. It's an odd time for family history, I'm bound to say. But quiet.' Lord Scattergood made the best of the matter. 'In fact, an uncommonly peaceful scene.'

This was incontestable. Arthur had drawn up on a stretch of grass by the roadside, and it was possible partly to see and partly to sense around them an empty countryside, slumbering snugly beneath its tidy coverlet of field and copse. It was very still when the purr of the engine faded. Arthur lowered the window beside him, for the car was still heavy with Mr Archdeacon's tobacco, faintly blended with a residual tap-room smell from Dr Rosenwald. Then he paused, arrested. 'Odd,' he said. 'Can you hear a bell?'

'A bell, Arthur?' Lord Scattergood shook his handsome head beneath its deerstalker. 'I can't say that I do. And who would want to ring a bell at an hour like this? Could it be people ringing one of those tiresome marathon peals at Abbot's Benison?'

Arthur leant out of the car. 'It's gone. Perhaps I imagined it. It wasn't like bell-ringing of that sort – more like an alarm bell.'

'Indubitably an auditory hallucination.' Mr Archdeacon, with his manuscript open before him, was impatient of this distraction. 'The delusive impression of hearing a bell-like note may be traced to acoustic laws which themselves depend upon the simple fact that the ear is a cartilaginous funnel. But of this I may speak on another occasion. Let me repeat: shall I begin?'

'By all means, Archdeacon. We are all attention. Arthur and myself, that is to say. Perhaps I had better wake up Rosenwald?'

'It is unnecessary – and might even be indiscreet. What I am to read is a good deal concerned with paintings, including what is incontestably the Leda of Titian. But if our Roman friend is to help us, it may be judicious to let him sleep as long as may be.'

'Clear-headed when he wakes up – eh?'

'Precisely. And – so far as the Leda is concerned, the better able to distinguish between a goose and a swan.' Mr Archdeacon paused to allow time for any merriment that this sally might provoke, and then cleared his throat. 'I proceed, then, to the diary of William Spendlove, first Earl of Scattergood, for the year 1720.'

# CHAPTER SIXTEEN

1720. 1 Aug. This Day my Son Rupert, together with his late *Companion de Voyage* and former Fellow at *Westminster School*, Jack Candleshoe, is safe returned from his Travels. Mr Drake, the Boys' worthy Tutor, declares them to be now perfect in *Latin* Verses (each indeed what Horace desired to be called, *Romanae fidicen Lyrae*) as well as largely exercised in the Mathematics and the several Branches of Natural Philosophy. That so much regular Instruction can have been combined with the *peripatetical* Part of their Education is a Thing to marvel at – if not to take, as my good Neighbour and Cousin Thomas Candleshoe doth aver, *cum granum salis*. The Conversation of both Lads at Dinner (to which I bade Squire Candleshoe and his Wife) was indeed edifying and learned to a gratifying and surprising Degree, with much Talk of large Collections – as alike of Books, Minerals, Plants, Antiquities both Classical and Gothick etc. – presently to follow them back from *Italy*. To all this deep Commerce with the *Muses* it is my own Hope that a decent Acquaintance with the *Graces* has been added; and that Rupert, whose Talk appeared to me to smell somewhat musty and of the Lamp, has equally improved himself in *le Ton de la bonne Compagnie*, and gained from his Wanderings those polished Manners and that *certaine Tournure* so necessary in the Station that he must (in the Fullness of Time) be called upon to fill and, if possible, adorn. I would have my dear Boy, above all Things, confirmed in the exactest moral Principles of a rationally believing Christian, as also of solid Knowledge and correct Judgement as to his intellectual Parts. It would be sadly vexatious however were he to turn out mere Parson or Pedant, fitter for the Laurels of a *College* and Plaudits of a *School* than for the just Esteem of the *Court* and *Senate* of his Country. Let honest Candleshoe's Boy aspire to slumber in some *Brasenose* Garret or *Christ Church* Stall. Rupert must consider that from simple *Earl* (a middle Station accordant with my own retired and unostentatious Temper) he is like to be *Duke* or *Marquess*; and learn to combine polite Learning and a fixed and unenthusiastick Piety with due Attention to Circumstance, Dignity, and the Bearing proper in the *magnificent* Man. (Aristot.)

1720. 8 Aug. Rupert continues in his learned Humour. At Dinner tonight somewhat tediously instructive on Optics and Astronomy. It now appears that at Padua he and Jack Candleshoe gave 80 *l* between them for a large optic Tube or *Telescope*, which is like to be delivered presently upon us. Talk of its being set up on the Leads etc. I fear we may be put under some Imputation of Singularity at *Benison* should this Extravagance of the Boys' go forward. They envisage, it appears, much nocturnal Experiment, with Observation of the Movement of Bodies etc.

1720. 12 Sept. In Town still. Supped with Richard Boyle, Son of my ever-lamented Friend, and was afterwards engaged in the Tour of *Burlington House,* now re-edified, enlarged, and adorned with great Curiosity and Taste by him. It is nothing so fine as *Benison*, but for a Town House well enough. His Ldship extremely polite in Expressions of Esteem for my dear Boy's Progress in the Sciences, and Command of the Mathematicals, curious Figures, etc. He spoke of making Interest for Rupert's Entrance into the *Royal Society*, the principal Body in the Kingdom for Persons expert in Natural Knowledge. Although R. Boyle be himself young I listened with Attention and Gratification, all of that Family being famous *Virtuosi* and well able to pronounce on Matters of the Sort. Returning by Coach to Scattergood House resolved to review more kindly Rupert's late Proposal for his *Solomon's Cottage* (as he and his Jack wd call it) beyond the Park. This Morning a Letter from Rupert respectfully urging Festination in my pronouncing upon the same, the Italian Books, Collections, Instruments, and the like being any Day expected now.

1720. 22 Sept. I find Squire Candleshoe to be not well disposed towards the Project of our two Lads for a learned Retreat of their own in the *Abbot's Lodging*. He thinks it were better that an Eye should be kept on them, and expresses himself as having small Confidence in the Perspicacity of Mr Drake. Since the Provision of this joint Tutor has been by a good Part more at my Charge than the Squire's, I have felt myself mightily inclined to take this ill, but have so far restrained any irascible Word in the Interest of neighbourly Feeling. I doubt whether one of inconsiderable Property and obscure Situation, such as is our good Squire, can readily be a Man of liberal Feeling or extensive Views.

1720. 23 Sept. A sultry Day, but with something of *Fraicheur* towards Evening. Took Advantage of this to stroll with Rupert to the *Abbot's Lodging*. The dear Boy again very eager for his Project, urging the Advantages of Seculsion, Retirement etc. in promoting those severer and more advanced Studies to which he and his Friend now wish to proceed. It appears that the Behaviour of *Venus* may in the coming Months be examined into with some special Prospect of learned Success. Rupert hath a Plan ready drawn out for the ready converting of the *Lodging* to this *Solomon's House* or *Cottage*. The Name whimsically derived from that curious Work *New Atlantis* by Sir F. Bacon, later First Viscount St Albans. Amusing Particulars from Rupert of many the first Nobles alike of *France* and *Italy* presently renowned as *Curiosi* and *Projectors*.

1720. 30 Oct. The Work on *Solomon's Cottage* far advanced. Sundry great Boxes and Crates, unopened here since their Arrival from *Leghorn*, have today gone down by Wagon to their new Abode. Rupert and his Jack in great Joy. For my own Part I take much delight in the Spectacle of two young Men, in whom their Years might licence some Wildness of Fancy if not of Behaviour, thus intent upon the Advancement of Learning. I recall with unaffected Contrition my own Youth, so sadly at Variance with this Sobriety, Usefulness and Good Sense. It is Mr Drake's Belief that a large Reform of youthful Morals and Manners hath been brought about by the Writings and Christian Example of Mr Joseph Addison, so unhappily deceased in the Course of the last Year. I have questioned Rupert on this, and find that he does modestly confess Mr Addison to be an Example indeed.

1720. 7 Nov. This Day was entertained to a Collation by my dear Son Rupert and his excellent Henchman Jack Candleshoe. The Dishes choice but very simple. We drank Water, and later an Infusion of Tea. Their Attendance is to be only one Lad, whom Rupert begged our good Mr Drake to choose upon the strictest Principles of settled Conduct and moral Probity. On the Ground Floor are convenient Offices for this Servant; a Study or Library, plainly furnished but commodious to the Labours of our young Philosophers; and two Sleeping Apartments in a simple Style, having no Ambition of Elegance. Thus it will be possible for the Boys to pernoctate from Time to Time, according to their astronomical Occasions. I highly approve these Dispositions, and Squire Candleshoe is at least so far reconciled to them as to withdraw any vocal Objections. He has offered, indeed, to install (the better to insure the Health and Comfort of our Lads) a motherly Person as Housekeeper and occasional Cook. But this the Boys have positively declined, having a set Fancy, it would appear, that *Solomon's Cottage* (like the *Abbot's Lodging* before it) should be wholly *celibate* and *monastical* in its Economy. Upon the upper Floor the Roof over one Apartment hath been removed, and the *Great Telescope* is (I suppose) by now there established. But of this Part of their Domain the Boys are jealous Guardians, and I have promised not to profane by any ignorant Inspection the Mysteries of their Science. It is to be hoped that Perkin (for such is the Denomination of their youthful Attendant) will occasionally be permitted to circulate in this higher Region with a Broom.

1720. 12 Dec. My dear Rupert's twentieth Birthday. Inquired of his Studies, at which, judging by his Absences, he hath been assiduous of late. He replied that he becomes steadily more absorbed in, and delighted with, the Heavenly Movements.

1721. 8 May. I write in the greatest Confusion of Mind and Agitation of Spirit. But let me compose myself, and be systematical. This a.m. early comes Squire Candleshoe in as vast Rage and Incoherence as I have ever known Man evince; and falls to imprecating *Benison* and all Spendloves that ever were in a Manner to be excused only as the Issue of plain Frenzy. Eventually somewhat subdued (if not mollified) by my own inflexible Exhibition of superior Breeding, he came within the Bounds of intelligible Sense. *Solomon's Cottage*, he declared, had its sole Affinity with Aught of that Monarch's only as a very Mark and Acme of amatorious and venereal Indulgence. Those *nocturnal Experiments* which our Boys had been pursuing in the Interests of *Natural Knowledge* –

Should these artless Pages ever, at some remote Time, come within the Notice of an other Eye than mine, will it not readily be understood that here the unhappy Writer dropped his Pen? But I continue now. The Lad Perkin, it appears, having received upon the Occasion of some casual Offence too hearty a Drubbing from his Masters, had allowed a Thirst for Vengeance and the Hope of Gain so far to suborn his Fidelity as to bring him before the Squire this very Morning with a substantial Account of a World of licentious Folly into which our miserable Boys have fallen. Of what followed let a bare Note suffice. The Squire (mounting whatever wretched Nag his Stables afforded him, and hastening to the Spot) was in Time to surprise, and drive out while yet in their Smocks, the particular *Heavenly Bodies* which had been engaging the *absorbed* and *delighted* Attention of our precious Couple, encouraging them, with a smart Thwack upon their ill-guarded Persons, to return to whatever *Orbit* is properly theirs in *Abbot's Benison* or *Benison Parva*. Having then assured the Reprobates of his unfeigned Regret that they were by some *two Summers* beyond the Reach of similar and more extended Castigation, the Squire rode straight on to *Benison Court*, his ill-directed and offensive Rage mounting in him as he approached. Our Interview, I verily believe, might well have come to the Point of Honour and an Affair of Rapiers, had I not steadfastly maintained all of the Reserve, judiciously tempered by Candour and Condescension, incumbent upon a *Peer* in a trying Situation.

I will not dwell further upon the Day's Scenes of Reprehension and Penitence. I have had at least the Satisfaction of knowing the sole feasible Procedure to adopt. With a Lad who has thus scandalously comported himself, *and been detected*, there is only one course to take. At three of the Clock this Afternoon Rupert departed with Mr Drake for the University, where he will at once be entered as a Nobleman of my own old College. I trust that his genuine Proficiency in Mathematical Study, if not that in *curious Figures*, will earn him the Regard of the resident Fellows, to whom I have strictly charged him to comport himself with Affability and a reasonably familiar Address. Rupert, I am willing to believe, is truly penitent; nor, after a World of Tears throughout the Morning, was I altogether displeased at his Mode of parting with me. Leaning from the Window of the Carriage, the Rogue had the Impertinence to murmur that, could but Peg (his detected Paphian Girl) make the Journey with him, it would be rounding off his astronomical Studies with *the Transit of Venus*.

1721. 12 May. Squire Candleshoe, it seems, has taken a Leaf out of my Book (which is indeed proper for him to do), and his Jack is packed off to Cambridge – not indeed with a Tutor of his own, but to be put under the Care of some worthy Tutor of a College. So here should be an End of this troublesome Affair. The Squire and I are to meet presently at *Solomon's Cottage* (to use the Name which, I fear, must ever adhere to it, at least in local Fame) and agree upon a proper Dispersal of whatever is unsuitably contained there. The Studies of these discreet (yet not sufficiently discreet) Boys have had, as it now appears, genuine Substance; and my Rupert (I suspect) was indeed something further advanced in the Courses of the veritable Planets than in his *sublunary* Researches. It thus seems not proper or convenient wholly to make away with what is of an authentick philosophic Cast in the Place. I apprehend little Possibility of serious Dispute with my good Neighbour, despite the high Tone of our last Encounter. Since the *Abbot's Lodging* is an undisputed Part of my own Estate, indeed, the Squire would be on but uncertain Ground were he minded to be disputatious.

1721. 16 May. All is in sad Confusion between Squire Candleshoe and me. I blame myself for taking up, over Matters of small Consideration in themselves, a Position from which it now appears difficult with any Dignity to recede. The Root of the Mischief lies in the good Squire's having allowed his Jack, during his Grand Tour made in Company with my Rupert and Mr Drake, a larger pecuniary Supply than was at all consonent with the Modesty of his Station. The Candleshoes have ever had a particular Pride or Arrogance in all their Associations with Spendloves – a Consequence of their being (what, as a Man of Candour, I have always been free to acknowledge) the elder Line of that Family from which our Antiquity is derived. This having led our honest Squire to dip deep into his Pocket on his itinerant Son's Behalf, Jack, it seems, hath on sundry Occasions disbursed more – as on other Occasions indubitably much less – than my own Boy upon those diverse Antiquities and Curiosities with the Acquiring of which the Lads liberally amused themselves upon their *Italian* Peregrination. These Objects they later disposed about their detestable *Cottage* in all the Carelessness of common Ownership, so that it is now scarce possible to make a just Appropriation or Assignment between them.

All this would seem, indeed, of little Moment but for a Circumstance at once flagitious and vexing. For preserving from parental Scrutiny the larger upper Apartment of their Dwelling the Boys now appear to have had this sufficient Reason, *viz*. that it had pleased them to appoint it with all Voluptuousness and amatory Luxury of *Venetian Houses* with which no modest Traveller through that carnal City would willingly hold the least Acquaintance. Once more my Pen would almost drop from my Fingers as I record this shameful fact – mitigated though it be (at least in some minor Degree) by the Observation (which my own sadly irregular Courses in early Life have enabled me to make) that Something more of Imagination than Familiarity hath gone to the framing of this most culpable Extravagance. But now to the Point at special Issue. Among the Embellishings of this rural *Bagnio* for simple Peg and Moll what have the Squire and I fallen upon but three large and erotical Paintings in Oil, *viz.* a Lollia Paulina, a Leda and Swan, and a Diana and Actaeon, all very rich in Colour and splendid in the Flesh – so much so, indeed, as to put the good Squire something out of Countenance, as having small Connoisseurship in graphick Immodesties. When however it did presently transpire that, while the Diana (although very brave with bathing Nymphs, and an Actaeon with his Stag's Head exceeding quaint) is by one Schiavone (a *Venetian* of small Regard), yet the Lollia and Leda are by that Tiziano Vecelli or Da Cadore now above all other *Italian* Artists hugely esteemed; when, I say, it appeared that our Boys had (at a great and notable Bargain) acquired two such *Canvasses* as the greatest *Curiosi* in the Kingdom might envy them the Luck of, then did Squire Candleshoe pipe to another Tune.

So here we are, my honest Neighbour and myself, at Jar together and by the Ears over these same Paintings, which is surely a bad Sequel to a worse Business. All this Afternoon did we debate the Matter, with Squire Candleshoe very hot – and outrageous, too, in Expression and Suggestion, as that *he should render me the Swan but allow me never a Collop of the Wench,* or that we had best cleave the Schiavone in twain, *himself to have the Ladies and myself to be well-suited by the Fellow with the Horns.* And thus are we parted with high Words and short Tempers; and Nothing settled betwixt us in a Matter that both Discretion and Decency cry aloud to see softly handled.

1721. 18 May. *The First Part of the Contention betwixt the Two Famous Houses of Candleshoe and Benison* (to *parody* the Title of the old Play) is now acted out and settled – and altogether to the Advantage of the younger Line. Yet while I rejoice at this Success, and at the just Castigation of the Insolence of my irascible Neighbour, I am yet apprehensive of the Scandal like to be spread (at least so far as the Boundaries of our County) by the wild Events of the last Night; and of suffering somewhat in my Dignity as *First Earl* by *un Eclat de rire* such as lively Rumours of the same may occasion.

And here I must unaffectedly confess (to the Privacy of this inviolate Page) that at my first Sight of Tiziano's Leda I did myself judge her a monstrous fine Woman (although so ill employed), and that his Lollia Paulina too appeared to me of a Rarity much excelling those Jewels with which the Painter (by a Licence to be reprobated from an *Ethick* Point of View) had alone adorned her. From this I was led to the Consideration that my Rupert, as a Lad from his earliest Years bred to the greatest Refinement and Politeness, as also to the Conversation of Women of the first Quality, was likelier by far than our good Squire's honest Jack to have been the original Appraiser, and consequent sole Purchaser, of these exalted Productions of a Master's Brush. When to this I added the further Thought, that the Objects of which the Property was thus disputed had been freely conveyed to, and now reposed in, a Building incontestably mine, and to which None have any Right or Title of Entrance save by my Leave, it did appear to me that the old Doctrine, whereby Possession is declared to be *nine-tenths of the Law*, might well be acted upon, and that with all Speed possible.

Thus it was that Yesterday (but biding my Time until Dusk, that the Matter might be carried through in a decent Privateness) I despatched Three or Four (such as were of a Discretion I could trust) with a Wagon to *Solomon's Cottage*, that they might bring these three Paintings (alike the Tizianos and the Schiavone, being itself, although less valuable, a sportive Work *d'un vrai Divertissement*) with all Haste and Quietness to Benison. For I made bold to think that, once hung in my Great Gallery or octagon room, there would be but small Hazard that those Trophies of my dear Boy's Purity of Taste (as I now saw it to be) would ever depart thence to an obscure Lodgement at Candleshoe.

But here was a Train of Reflection upon which *Two* might fall. And thus came it about that my Servants, proceeding at my Command upon this lawful Occasion, were at the *Cottage* hotly encountered by a like Number of Squire Candleshoe's Men, most nefariously and thievishly furnished with a Wagon to an identical Purpose with mine. Thence followed a notable Skirmish, with diverse bloody Cockscombs and (I fear) at least one broken Crown – the Hurly-burly receiving vast Increase (ere all was over) from several Reinforcements on either Side gathered from the nearer Villages. Yet out of all this great Disgrace (as Persons of any civil Breeding must unfeignedly conceive it) has come this fair Conclusion: that while the worthy Squire indeed has escaped away with the Schiavone and certain other Paintings of little or no Name, my dear Rupert's more truly inspired Purchases (the Leda and the Lollia of Tiziano, to wit) are now safe within the Portals of Benison. This Morning, it is true, being something too incensed by the Temerity of my Neighbour, I took Horse for Candleshoe, intent to demand that the third Painting be lawfully rendered me. But finding the Squire (who had been advised of my Approach) standing to Arms upon his Threshold, with a most martial Levy of his Retainers arrayed behind him, and himself crying out that *did I want the horned Fellow a-peeping at the Ladies, I might come in and find him*, I judged it well to speak him fair, and as if turning the Matter to a notable Jest. For it would be an inconvenient Thing, if Cognizance of all this were taken by some officious Justice; and it could be said that *a Nobleman and a Gentleman of the County had been summoned to keep the Peace together, after coming to Blows over the Spoils of a detected Bawdy-house.*

1721. 30 May. Caused to be hung in my Great Gallery my two new-acquired Paintings by Tiziano Vecelli (formerly styled Da Cadore), being that Artist commonly reckoned by the Curious first among all those out of *Italy*. Both mighty fine, and in the Leda I do begin to perceive a great Sweetness in the Expression, as also *une certaine Rondeur des Fesses*, that alike do most charmingly remind me of my Ever-to-be-Honoured Mother's Maid, Betty Brown, the first that I well remember to have –

But here Company obliges me to lay down my Pen. *Une belle Assemblée* is like to be with us this Evening, and I propose no small Pleasure to myself in my two new Evidences of that Correct Taste and those Liberal Expenditures which steadily enhance the Elegance of *Benison Court*.

# CHAPTER SEVENTEEN

'If that isn't a deuced queer thing.' As Mr Archdeacon finished his reading, and as Arthur Spendlove let in his clutch with what in a less seasoned car would have been a jerk, Lord Scattergood spoke with some emphasis. 'I'm quite sure I never heard this yarn before.'

'Precisely.' Mr Archdeacon paused to get his pipe in commission. 'It is only lately, as you know, that I have come to work through the first earl's papers. Had these circumstances been known to me in 1939 – '

'You wouldn't have handed back this disputed property to the Candleshoes on a plate.' Arthur chuckled. 'What mugs they must have thought us. Supposing, that is, they knew.'

'They must have known, Arthur, or they would scarcely have played this trick on us.' Lord Scattergood, conscious in this of a large stroke of intellectual clarity, banged so vigorously on the seat in front of him that Dr Rosenwald for a brief moment came awake again. 'But, my dear Archdeacon, did the old girl *behave* as if she knew? Can you recall anything to suggest that those particular paintings meant something to her?'

'I cannot say that I do. Miss Candleshoe was concerned to drive a bargain in point of what she was to store for us; and she was not without acuteness in the matter of insurance. But in the particular works involved, and their qualities, she appeared not interested. It was, I fear, her attitude that nothing from Benison was likely to be of the first quality. All this, however, may well have been dissimulation. Miss Candleshoe may well have been gloating inwardly at the strange opportunity our proposal was bringing her.'

'Gloating?' A just indignation was evidently beginning to rise in Lord Scattergood. 'I'd call that a shocking thing, you know – a most unneighbourly thing.'

'I agree with you, Marquess. We must remember, however, that Squire Candleshoe must have formed just such a judgement upon the Earl's conduct in 1721. It is only too probable, I fear, that Miss Candleshoe, a woman of strong family piety, as she contemplated the Leda and the Lollia, reflected that thus the whirligig of time brings in his revenges.'

'That her chance had come – eh?'

'It must be entertained as a tenable hypothesis. On the other hand, Miss Candleshoe may be blameless. And I have myself little to go upon, since my commerce with her upon the relevant occasion was restricted and indeed inconsiderable. I dealt in the main with a housekeeper – an unusual woman, whom I have cause to remember with some particularity. She died, I believe, very shortly after. I wondered at the time whether I ought – But that is another story. And now a fresh consideration presents itself to me. Armigel.'

'Eh?'

'There was then – as there is now – living with Miss Candleshoe a retired clergyman of the name of Armigel. He acted as a domestic chaplain.'

'Services on the spot and as required? The sort of thing we bring in the Bishop for from time to time?' Lord Scattergood was impressed. 'Arthur – do you hear that? Dashed convenient notion.'

'But mark.' Mr Archdeacon, as he delivered himself of this injunction, turned round and pointed the stem of his pipe at his employer. 'Not the present employment of Armigel, but rather something that I now recall of his first profession, is the circumstance to which some large significance may well attach. Let me be brief.'

As Arthur heard these ominous words he swung the car

off the high road between two unimpressive stone columns. 'Capital! For here we are.'

'Let me be *very* brief. Armigel's first profession was that of artist. He was a painter – although I believe an undistinguished one.'

'Then that settles it!' Lord Scattergood's righteous wrath was now given unrestricted issue. 'This scoundrel copied our Titians at his leisure; and substituted his beastly efforts for the real thing, when the time came to send them back to Benison. Upon my soul, if he wasn't a clergyman, I'd have him sent to gaol.'

'You'd be laughed at for your pains.' Arthur spoke with conviction. 'The whole story of Solomon's Cottage would come out, and then ... ' Arthur broke off abruptly, and braked so hard that they were all thrown forward in their seats. 'Something's fallen across the drive. It's a tree.' He switched off his engine. 'We can't get any farther.'

'Then we must get out and walk.' Lord Scattergood's vein of high lucidity held. 'Archdeacon, my dear fellow, I'm sorry to give you this inconvenience. But we must decidedly go right ahead.'

'By all means Marquess. There is small hardship in a brief nocturnal perambulation on such a night. But what of our Roman friend?'

Lord Scattergood, as he prepared to step from the car, gave Dr Rosenwald an experimental shake. 'Leave him behind – eh Arthur? Send for him if we want him.'

'Just that.' Arthur was already scrambling over the fallen tree. 'The house isn't a quarter of a mile.'

'Then it should all be plain sailing.' Lord Scattergood lent a solicitous arm to his librarian as he in turn negotiated the obstacle. 'We present ourselves, explain that the imposture is detected, and take the Titians quietly home with us. No need to admit that it has made us a bit hot under the collar – what?'

'An admirable proposal, Marquess. As your politic

ancestor put it, restrain any irascible word in the interest of neighbourly feeling.'

Arthur allowed himself a sceptical laugh. 'And hope that Miss Candleshoe will be subdued, if not mollified, by an inflexible exhibition of superior breeding? Well, we can only try. And good humour will certainly be the note on which to begin.'

'I don't anticipate any trouble.' A mood of confidence appeared to grow in the rightful owner of the Leda and the Lollia as he trudged up the neglected and moonlit drive towards Candleshoe. 'Lucky that we have come by night, you know. Less chance of gossip. A firm line and – believe me – everything will go off very quietly.'

'It is certainly very quiet now.' Mr Archdeacon spoke almost dreamily from amid his cloud of tobacco. 'The imagination of a poet could scarcely propose to itself a scene of more unflawed tranquillity. See, my dear Marquess, how sweet the moonlight sleeps upon this bank! It will be within the scope of your recollection that Shakespeare – '

Abruptly, Mr Archdeacon's discourse broke off. For on this so tranquil night another voice had made itself heard. It was close at hand, and its tone was uncompromising.

'*Stand quite still. I have a gun, and I can drop any two of you.*'

# CHAPTER EIGHTEEN

'Now, what would be the meaning of that?' Lord Scattergood stops and peers ahead with considerable interest. The moonlight, although doubtless sleeping upon banks much as at Belmont, is an uncertain and low-powered affair, so that it is difficult to distinguish much. Just ahead, the drive appears to take one of its numerous twists and disappear into shadows. It is from this obscurity that the voice has spoken, and now it speaks again. Loud but level, it conveys every impression of intending business.

*'I mean to continue getting right out of this. You can surround me, you can outflank me, you can rush me. But I can get two of you, or perhaps three, before you get me. So that may mean any of you – get that? Maybe it would be healthier if you were to quit.'*

Lord Scattergood moves on again. 'Odd – eh? What would you make of it, Arthur?'

'I suppose we are being addressed by one of the fellows who were so interested in the paintings when Archdeacon was showing people round. They are here before us, sure enough. What would you say, Archdeacon?'

'I am in agreement with you, Lord Arthur. We are indubitably being addressed by a criminal. ... How treacherous the surface of this drive is! In this uncertain light it is positively dangerous.'

*'You've been warned. Stop, or I drop you dead.'*

'Incompetent – what?' Lord Scattergood shakes his deer-stalker in the moonlight. 'If he wants to get away, why keep shouting at us? Sounds almost as if attracting attention was his idea.'

'It rather does.' Arthur is puzzled.

'Well, he shall get it.' Lord Scattergood speaks with

some asperity, and quickens his pace. 'Let me just catch sight of him, and I shall tell him precisely what I think.'

'*It's your last chance. I tell you to stop.*'

'Indubitably what is called a gangster.' Mr Archdeacon pronounced this with assurance. 'The accent is decisive. I have frequently heard it in the cinema.'

'American?' Lord Scattergood is much interested. 'And proposing to smuggle my paintings out of the country – eh? And there he is!'

They have rounded a bend. Before them, uncertainly visible in shadow, is the stationary figure of a man. Arthur has a momentary impression – which further puzzles him – that the man has his back to them and is addressing vacancy. But, if this is so, he immediately swings round. There is no doubt that he has a gun, and that they are covered by it.

'Stop!'

Lord Scattergood, who is now much incensed, replies to this with a snort of indignation and stumps on. At his side, Mr Archdeacon has all the appearance of emitting a smokescreen to cover this advance. Arthur tries to get ahead of them, but has no success. His father, having got within a dozen paces of the waiting man, feels that the time has come to offer a few remarks. 'You miserable rascal!' he says. 'Terrorizing a helpless old woman! I'll have you know that the lady is my kinswoman, and moreover has the custody of some of my most valuable possessions. I respect her highly, you scoundrel; and if you think I'll permit antics like yours on her property – why, you're a very great donkey!' Lord Scattergood, as he finishes this address, comes within arm's length of the gangster and knocks his gun from his hand.

'Say – aren't you the Marquess?' The gangster – he is a young man of dishevelled but polite appearance – asks this question in what, to Arthur, is patent bewilderment.

'I am Lord Scattergood. But your business in the

immediate future, you horrible ruffian, is going to be with the police.'

'And you said something about Miss Candleshoe having valuable possessions of yours?'

'My Titians, rascal – as you very well know.'

'Paintings? Then that's what they're after!'

At this Arthur steps forward. 'What's that?'

'The thieves, sir – the folk I've been trying to lead off.'

'I see.' Arthur takes a keen look at the young man, stoops and picks up the fallen gun. 'Loaded?'

'No. We got it from one of them in a fight, but it wasn't loaded. I brought it out and started doing what I could to get their attention. That was so that a boy from the house – a boy called Robin – could get past them, and bring help from the village. You see, Candleshoe is besieged. There's quite a crowd of those crooks. . . . Perhaps I ought to say that my name is Grant Feather.'

Lord Scattergood, who had listened to this with attention, turns to his librarian. 'Archdeacon, what are we to make of this?'

'Granted the given terms of our present situation, Marquess, the problem of the young man's veracity would appear, for the time, to be unamenable to other than a purely empirical approach.'

'Go ahead, but keep an eye open – what?' And Lord Scattergood nods understandingly before turning back to the young man. 'You been inside Candleshoe?'

'Yes, sir. And my mother's there right now.'

'Seen my Titians – Lollia somebody, and an odd girl with a swan?'

'I just don't get that, Lord Scattergood. I saw those paintings at Benison today – or I suppose I ought to say yesterday afternoon.'

'You saw copies of them. The originals have been st –' Lord Scattergood checked himself at a warning cough from Mr Archdeacon. 'The originals, for reasons into which I need not enter, have been for some time at Candleshoe. And now it appears that a pack of rascals are after them. You haven't seen them – either hung up or stored away?'

'No, sir – nor heard them mentioned either. But Candleshoe is quite a big place. And what you say does explain things. These people are much more likely to be after a couple of valuable paintings than a pirate hoard hidden in a secret chamber.'

'A pirate hoard? Stuff and nonsense.'

'That's what Jay thinks it is.'

Arthur Spendlove interposes. 'Jay? Who is he?'

'A capable kid who lives with Miss Candleshoe. His name is Jay Ray.'

From the base of what is now a tall column of tobacco smoke Mr Archdeacon emits a sound of mild interest. 'Ray? Surely there cannot be – '

'Quite right, Archdeacon. No boy could be called Jay Ray. The idea's absurd.' And Lord Scattergood looked with renewed suspicion at Grant Feather. 'And as for a pirate – '

'My dear Marquess, you misconstrue the sense of my proposed observation. But no matter. Suffice it to remark that an *American* boy might conceivably have such a name.'

Grant Feather laughs at this. 'He's American, all right. But – what's more important – he's all alone in Candleshoe now, with the two old folk, and my mother, and a bunch of children younger than himself. And these crooks may be starting another attack.'

'Then we'd better be moving on.' It is Arthur Spendlove who speaks, and he steps out as he does so. 'What about that other boy – Robin, did you say? Will he have reached the village?'

'Not yet. But he sure will quite soon. I'm certain he got clean away.'

'Then there doesn't seem much to worry about. We'll go up to the house now, and wait for the arrival of the police, and so on. With a crowd of us like this, it isn't likely that the thieves will show up again. They certainly don't seem much in evidence at the moment.' Arthur turns to Grant. 'Don't you think they may have gone already? For I gather you didn't actually draw them when you put up that diversionary turn?'

'I did not. And it makes me a mite uneasy. I think they feel they've got a trump card, and believe they can play it any moment now. That would account for their not much minding whether I walked straight out of the place or not. They reckon that they can be clear of Candleshoe, Titians and all, before any effective force can be mustered.'

'In that case, Mr Feather, they are wrong.' Lord Scattergood delivers himself of this with a snort of indignation, and at the same moment quickens his pace. 'My son and I, together with Mr Archdeacon ... By the way, this is Mr Archdeacon.'

'How do you do, sir.'

'How do you do.'

'I say that my son and I, together with Mr Archdeacon and yourself, constitute an effective force in ourselves. Archdeacon, am I wrong?'

'Certainly not, Marquess. No other view of the matter would occur to me. We have all the makings of a well-balanced force, if I may say so.'

'Precisely.' And now from under his deerstalker Lord Scattergood turns a stern eye on Grant. 'You, sir – do you agree?'

At this – and with a deplorable lack of military caution – Grant gives a shout of laughter. 'Yes, Marquess. But we're nothing on the garrison at present in the house, or I'd never have quit it, even to get that boy away. If we can get in and join up with it, we should do pretty well.

But you will have to take your orders from Jay.'

'From the boy? Does Miss Candleshoe do that?'

Grant laughs again. 'When there's a crisis, I guess she treats him pretty well as commander-in-chief.'

'Then – while we are inside Candleshoe – that settles the matter.' Having thus declared himself, Lord Scattergood continues to march up the drive. 'Would it be the sort of place that has a front-door bell?'

'I suppose so.' Grant finds this an odd question. 'Wouldn't Benison have a front-door bell?'

'Do you know, I've never looked to see?' Lord Scattergood appears much struck by this circumstance. 'But here we are. And no doubt the best thing will be a very loud knock.'

Candleshoe is before them, and Grant sees that the moon has moved on as if to inspect a fresh face of it. He has little idea of the time, but knows that the small hours have come. Even so, he could count the hours of his acquaintance with the house very readily upon his ten fingers. And this is strange, since it already has the air of an established landmark in his life. Moreover he is still apprehensive that it may have come to stay. The night's wild events, when happily over, will by no means render the place less endearing in his mother's regard. Miss Candleshoe and Mr Armigel, he gloomily reflects, may be water-colour sketching upon the Yang-tse-kiang within a twelve-month. Meanwhile he remembers Jay and his archers within, and the uncertain number of evilly – as it may be of desperately – disposed persons without. The approach to Candleshoe has its hazards, and he wonders whether Lord Scattergood ought to be apprised of them. 'Do you think, sir,' he presently asks, 'that the front door will be the best thing?'

'My dear fellow, nothing else would be civil. I have some business – family business, you might say – to discuss with Miss Candleshoe; and she is both a spirited woman and apt to stand upon old-fashioned forms. It wouldn't do to climb in through a bathroom window, you know – it wouldn't do at all. ... I think we go up these steps. Spot of mortar wouldn't come amiss to them – eh?'

They climb the steps. Grant doesn't at all know what is going to happen – a cloud of arrows from one direction or a rain of revolver bullets from another. But Lord Scattergood, who appears unable to command more than an intermittent consciousness of the altogether abnormal state of affairs at Candleshoe, is not a person with whose views one ought hastily to express nervous dissent; and Grant mounts the steps beside him. He can hear Mr Archdeacon, who is immediately behind, offering Arthur Spendlove miscellaneous antiquarian observations on the building. They are standing before the front door, and Lord Scattergood has found a knocker. In a moment Grant is realizing how deep has been the silence which the Marquess now proceeds to break. It is hard to believe that the enemy still lurks. It is even hard to believe that there has ever really been an enemy at all. The fantastic fracas in the library might be remembered from a broken dream.

'Who goes there?'

There is no doubt about what the garrison feels. The challenge, although its pitch suggests one of the less mature of Jay's following, rings out sharply and formidably enough. Lord Scattergood however comports himself as if his knock had produced a butler bowing gravely at an opened portal. 'Is Miss Candleshoe at home? The Marquess of Scattergood.'

There is silence for some seconds, during which Grant has an impression of considerable confabulation in progress behind the massive timber confronting them. And then comes the voice of Mr Armigel. It is placid and decisive. 'Miss Candleshoe is not at home.'

Grant's sense of the incongruity of this exchange is suddenly sharpened by the impression that he can hear voices somewhere in the darkness behind him. And they are not voices, somehow, that he can associate with the advance of any forces of law and order. In the circumstances Lord Scattergood's approach seems to him a little on the formal side. Moreover that nobleman, a moment before so resolute in manner, appears to be somewhat at a loss. It is only after a discernible hesitation that he makes a further move. 'In that case, and since I have business of some importance with her, I will just step in and write a note.'

Inside the house this produces further distinguishable conference. Outside, Grant is now sure that he hears not only voices but some sort of engine as well. He is trying to place this – it is not at all a familiar sound – when Mr Armigel delivers himself once more with the same placidity and decision. 'Miss Candleshoe regrets that her health disables her at present from holding either epistolatory or any other form of correspondence with her friends.'

For a moment this has all the appearance of being victoriously unanswerable. Lord Scattergood is reduced to turning round for the purpose of consulting his librarian. Grant turns too, and finds that he is looking over the heads of the others at a stretch of neglected lawn upon which the moon is now casting lengthening shadows. Something moves on it – something at first merely puzzling, and then unbelievable and monstrous. ... Grant takes one further look, swings round again, and shouts lustily. 'Jay! Are you there? Open up!'

'Grant?' Jay's voice comes from somewhere overhead.

'Make them open up. There's another attack coming. No time to lose.'

# CHAPTER NINETEEN

AMONG the more recent ancestresses of Mrs Feather – those active since the year 1620 – have been not a few ladies with the knack of continuing to keep things tidy while their husbands and sons have been shooting through the windows. It is doubtless this tradition that has prompted her, during the past hour or so, to encourage and assist the half-witted Tib to wash up. And to this in turn is due the fortunate circumstance that Miss Candleshoe is now able to receive her visitors in a great hall the feudal disorder of which is not incongruously enhanced by the remains of rabbit-pie and baked apples.

Mrs Feather is relieved to see Grant again, although she discerns at once that he is far from feeling this obscure nocturnal crisis to be over. Grant indeed no sooner appears than he vanishes once more, together with Jay and a middle-aged man whom she recognizes as Lord Arthur Spendlove. For the moment, therefore, Lord Scattergood is unaccompanied except by an ancient person, approximately coeval with Mr Armigel, who is occupied – very properly – in hastily stuffing away an enormous pipe as he advances into Miss Candleshoe's presence. Mrs Feather has, of course, no notion of the inwardness of the situation. Dimly, she supposes that Lord Scattergood – conceivably in his capacity as Lord-Lieutenant of the County – has arrived at the head of a troop of horse to the relief of his beleaguered neighbour. But this impression lasts only for a moment. Being a woman of swift perceptions, Mrs Feather quickly realizes that she is present at a clash of mighty opposites, and that the shades of Candleshoes and Spendloves innumerable may well be looking down upon the scene. Indeed, she can almost discern them at an impalpable jostle in the minstrels' gallery. This being so,

Mrs Feather further feels that she herself ought to assume some role significant for the occasion. Lord Scattergood is attended by the old person with the pipe; Miss Candleshoe – a circumstance, this, surely more impressive in itself – is flanked by her domestic chaplain; Mrs Feather sees that she herself is indubitably what is called a waiting gentlewoman, and she at once takes up on Miss Candleshoe's other hand a posture as evocative of this condition as she can contrive. She flatters herself that this makes Lord Scattergood start at a disadvantage.

And certainly Lord Scattergood is embarrassed. He begins by proffering Miss Candleshoe a good-evening – an anachronous tender to which the old lady replies only with one of her alarming bows. So alarming is it, indeed, that Lord Scattergood leaps forward with chivalrous haste and the evident object of fielding her neatly from the carpet. The discovery that this is an unnecessary solicitude puts him somewhat out of countenance, and he breaks abruptly into speech. 'I say, you know – my Leda and Lollia. It really won't do.'

Miss Candleshoe draws herself up. 'Lord Scattergood, I can well believe that you are in trouble again with your bitches. But need I be concerned in the matter?'

'Bitches, Miss Candleshoe?' Lord Scattergood is scandalized and bewildered.

'I presume that Leda and Lollia *are* bitches?'

'God bless my soul! Leda's a woman, Miss Candleshoe; and Lollia is too.'

'Ah – forgive me. I had supposed your concern was over *canine* bitches. My late brother, Sir James, frequently remarked to me that you had no happiness whatever with hounds. But if you are in trouble with *women*, Lord Scattergood, is there between us that degree of intimacy which would justify your appealing to *me*?'

It seems to Mrs Feather that Lord Scattergood, who is a florid man, is possibly going to suffer a stroke. He merely, however, turns to his companion. 'Archdeacon, will you be so good as to take this matter over? I'm damned if I can trust myself to say at all the proper thing.'

'Certainly, Marquess. Miss Candleshoe, let me be brief. It must be within the scope – '

'On second thoughts, I think I'll carry on myself.' Lord Scattergood thus changes his mind with what, to Mrs Feather, is inexplicable haste. 'The plain fact, ma'am, is that I've come for my Titians. So, I understand, have some rascally thieves who have also traced them here. We needn't – need we? – go at all deeply into the affair. Just take it that the time has come for the Titians to go back to Benison.' Lord Scattergood pauses hopefully, and then a further inspiration comes to him. 'And if you'd care yourself to have those deuced good copies – '

But Miss Candleshoe has turned to her chaplain. 'Mr Armigel,' she says, 'do my ears deceive me?'

'I fear not.' Mr Armigel is polishing his spectacles, as if preparatory to some distasteful but necessary scrutiny of the visitors. 'I fear that Lord Scattergood has appeared at this extraordinary hour for the sole purpose of putting forward an extravagant claim to the Candleshoe Titians. The paintings he has in mind appear to be those of which copies are well known to be exhibited at Benison. Lord Scattergood, in fact, has fallen into some sad confusion in this matter. Should he care to return at some more convenient time, I shall be happy to clear it up for him with the aid of the relevant family documents.'

'Family documents!' Mr Archdeacon at this can no longer contain himself; he produces his pipe and waves it wildly in the air. 'May I ask, sir, if you are aware of the existence of the personal journals of William Spendlove, first Earl of Scattergood, in which the provenance of the Titians – '

'And are you, Mr Archdeacon, familiar with the Candleshoe Papers?'

'The Candleshoe Papers? Certainly not! I never heard of them.'

'Precisely. They show conclusively that in the year 1721 Squire Candleshoe very properly took over the custody of certain Italian paintings which had been acquired by his son – '

'Nonsense, sir – contemptible nonsense! You know very well that the Earl carried off the paintings to Benison.'

'So the Earl thought.' Mr Armigel, conceivably because his invention is flagging, pauses to take a pinch of snuff. 'In point of fact, the Squire defeated the tiresome importunity of the Earl by permitting him to make off with two indifferent copies. I was most interested in the copies, Mr Archdeacon, when you sent them to be stored here during the war.'

'Lies, sir – impudent and impotent lies!' Mr Archdeacon is now considerably more florid than his employer. 'No forgeries existed, as you very well know, until you yourself took dastardly advantage of being entrusted with the originals, and exploited your previous profession in order to perpetrate a disgraceful fraud. You copied the Titians, sent copies back to us, and are concealing the originals in this house now. ... Bless me – what was that?'

It is not without due occasion – Mrs Feather has to acknowledge – that the Marquess of Scattergood's librarian thus abruptly suspends his doubtless just denunciation of Miss Candleshoe's domestic chaplain. A tremendous concussion has shaken the house to its massive foundations; a cloud of dust has risen from the floor; and from the wainscotted walls there is now tumbling and clattering a generous assortment of paintings, pikes, muskets, boars' heads, and suits of armour. A second concussion follows the first, and this is too much for a considerable portion of the elaborate plaster ceiling, which promptly deposits itself to the extent of a ton or so of debris just behind the spot upon which Lord Scattergood and Mr Archdeacon are standing.

Mrs Feather supposes an earthquake, and feels a sharp resentment that providence should thus visit Candleshoe when it appears to be within her grasp. As the dust disperses she sees the extent of the damage already occasioned, and reckons that a third or fourth tremor must bring down the whole tottering edifice in ruin. Mr Archdeacon, she notices, is behaving in an extraordinary way; he has picked up one of the fallen pikes and thrust it within the hands of Lord Scattergood; and now, with surprising agility, he is similarly providing himself with a broadsword and a shield. Thus equipped, Mr Archdeacon has all the appearance of a mythological personage addressing himself to the affair with the gods. Mrs Feather is a good deal impressed by this manner of taking arms against a natural visitation. Mr Archdeacon's defiance, however – which now takes the form of a bellow of rage – proves to be directed not against the heavens but against the Candleshoe faction as it still confronts him. The librarian, in fact, is under the impression that he and his employer have been the specific object of lethal attack by some monstrous engine; and he is proposing, at the sword's point, to seek immediate satisfaction. His advance upon Mr Armigel with this intent is only prevented by a third tremedous impact, followed by the sudden reappearance of Lord Arthur Spendlove, who shouts at his father across the hall.

'*They've got a tank!*'

This announcement – as might be expected – commands attention and a moment's silence. Lord Scattergood sets his pike carefully against the wall. 'A tank, my dear boy? Who have a tank?'

'The thieves – the fellows who are after our pictures.'

'Nonsense, Arthur. They can't have a tank. Such

things simply aren't sold. You cause Miss Candleshoe unnecessary alarm.'

'Didn't you hear it? They're using it to break into the library, which is less massive than the older parts of the house. And you don't need to buy a tank. You simply borrow one. At this time of year they are parked all over the place.'

'I call that a very scandalous thing. I shall take the matter up with the War Office.' Lord Scattergood reaches for his pike again, and then addresses Miss Candleshoe. 'Fortunately, ma'am, my boy here knows a thing or two about tanks. Played about with them a lot in the desert. Can show us the vulnerable spots, you know. Just let me get this through a slit' – and Lord Scattergood flourishes his weapon with fine confidence – 'and – by gad! – I'll tickle them up a bit. . . . There they go again.'

It is true that Candleshoe has taken yet another pounding. This time, a substantial piece of timber comes down virtually on Mr Armigel's toes. He looks at it in mild perplexity and turns to Miss Candleshoe. 'There can be little doubt that we are confronted with some obscure and untoward situation. Would it be prudent, I wonder, to send for Jay?'

'Certainly we must send for Jay.' Miss Candleshoe is uncompromising. 'Jay will compose this uproar, and assist the gentlemen from Benison to bed.'

'To bed?' Mr Armigel is puzzled.

'Precisely. There can be no doubt whatever that they are in liquor. Even a Spendlove, one supposes, would scarcely break in upon a neighbour and behave in this destructive manner when sober. Drink, as my late brother Sir James used frequently to remark, has been the curse of that family. But that is no more than justice. For is it not well known that their fortunes were founded upon bottling ditch-water?'

Lord Scattergood and Mr Archdeacon, who have alike

listened with mounting indignation to these monstrous aspersions, are plainly collecting themselves for spirited reply when Grant Feather runs into the hall. Arthur Spendlove turns to him. 'It's bad?'

'I'll say it is. They've got a mullion down, and they're almost through. Jay says our best chance is to get up to the Long Gallery and hold the stair-heads. His friend Robin must have made the village some time ago, and help should be arriving pretty soon.'

'Then up we go . . . Is this Jay?'

Jay had indeed followed Grant into the hall. The lantern he is carrying shows that his pallor has yielded to a faint flush. Mrs Feather suddenly sees in him a child who ought to have been tucked up and asleep hours ago. But Jay, if exhausted, has lost nothing of his peremptory manner. 'Will you all, please, go straight up to the gallery at once? It's the only part of the house we can now hope to hold.' Having given this general direction, Jay walks straight on to Mr Armigel. 'What is this, please, about two valuable pictures?'

'Pictures, Jay?' Thus challenged, the chaplain appears for the first time discomfited.

'They say we are hiding two valuable old paintings, and that the thieves want them. Is this true?'

'My dear Jay, this is a complicated matter. But it is true that we have – um – thought proper to detain at Candleshoe two paintings by Titian – a famous artist of whom you have doubtless heard – since their ownership is a circumstance of some family complication.'

'Nothing of the sort.' Mr Archdeacon breaks in with high indignation. 'The Marquess's title to the Titians is as plain as one of those pike-staffs.'

'Where are the pictures now, please?'

'Now, Jay?'

'If we are to defend them, they must go with us to the Long Gallery this instant. I can't guarantee another three minutes.' At this, the commander of Candleshoe produces from some fold of his sombre garments a schoolboy's large and innocent watch. 'So choose.'

Mr Armigel hesitates – whereupon Lord Scattergood steps forward. 'Where are the pictures, sir? Dash it all – would you have them go out of the family altogether, and be sold by a pack of thieves to some rascal in New York or Chicago?'

This well-calculated appeal has its effect. Mr Armigel glances at Miss Candleshoe, who almost imperceptibly nods. Then he turns back to Lord Scattergood. 'The Candleshoe Titians? They are, in point of fact, lying at your feet. They tumbled from the wall not five minutes ago.' Mr Armigel pauses to observe the effect produced by this startling intelligence, and is so heartened by what he sees as to break into a chuckle. 'For the sake of decency and reticence, my dear Marquess, I have thought proper a little to obscure them beneath a sound brown varnish. The Leda might be a goose girl, and you can hardly discern that the Lollia is disrobed. But underneath, I assure you, the work of Titian will be found, wholly unimpaired.'

Lord Scattergood opens his mouth at this – but nobody is ever to know what observation he is proposing to make. Another and even more violent concussion is followed by a sound of falling masonry, the shouts of children, and footsteps in rapid withdrawal towards the hall. Mr Archdeacon, with a nicely balanced chivalry and sense of property, seizes the Leda with one hand and Miss Candleshoe with the other. Lord Scattergood snatches up the Lollia, Mr Armigel takes a lantern, and Grant and Arthur grab weapons for the purpose of fighting a rearguard action. Jay vanishes in the direction in which Candleshoe has been breached, intent upon rallying his forces and achieving an orderly retreat. In a twinkling the great hall is empty – or empty save for the wolf-hound Lightning, who has so far evinced singularly little interest in the night's proceedings. And now Lightning, who has been lying in front of the empty fireplace, rises, yawns, stretches, and proceeds at leisure to join the perturbed humans now pounding and puffing their way upstairs to the Long Gallery.

# CHAPTER TWENTY

THE defence of this last fastness of Candleshoe is clearly a subject to which Jay has given considerable thought. The east staircase has been effectively sealed off long ago; here an attacker from below will finally be presented with a flat ceiling, the upper surface of which is so weighted with miscellaneous lumber that there is no possibility of forcing a way through it. The west staircase, up which the defenders have retreated, is left free and open. But a barricade has been moved into place at the top; and from this and from the uppermost landing the three final turns of the stair can be commanded by bowmen. It looks almost impregnable against any common assault. But Jay explains that there is a second line of defence. Should the stair-head have to be yielded, his force will retreat to the cover of the little stage at the east end of the gallery. From this position their bows will command what is virtually a long empty tunnel up which the enemy must advance. While their arrows last, and while they retain, too, a sufficiency of torches to cast some light upon the scene, they cannot be rushed without having the chance to inflict what ought to be annihilating casualties.

All this seems to Grant Feather to be a satisfactory state of affairs – and so is Jay's announcement that he has sent his two youngest retainers to light and stoke a beacon on the roof. If the outer world is hesitating over what to make of Robin's story – and it has occurred to Grant that it may well bear the appearance of implausible fantasy – the sight of this distant minor conflagration may well be a useful stimulant. Jay's confidence in Robin seems to extend to Robin's father, whom he judges certain to arrive with overwhelming forces long before these are seriously needed. Jay opens a window which he declares to command a distant view of the high road, and bids another henchman keep strict watch there for a long line of rapidly approaching cars. Grant wonders if Jay is quite as confident as he seems. It is certain that he has a flair for keeping up morale.

The tremendous blows upon the fabric of the building have ominously ceased, and there can be no doubt that the enemy now has the run of the house. But for a few minutes there is a lull in the gallery, and this usefully contributes to the composure of the company there assembled. Lord Scattergood and Miss Candleshoe, whom the pressure of events within the last fifteen minutes has impelled with miraculous speed to an appearance of unflawed family solidarity, are conversing in front of that odd alternative version of Admiral Candleshoe's monument which goes by the name of the Christmas box. Miss Candleshoe pokes at it here and there with her ebony stick – possibly by way of emphasizing its artistic merits, or possibly with the vague notion of touching off the spring that shall send it flying magically open. Lord Scattergood, who is shrewdly convinced that there will be no more trouble over the Titians, and who is by nature incapable of a flicker of discomposure in face of any number of rascals and ruffians, shows high good humour. Mr Archdeacon, who has stowed away the Leda and the Lollia behind a pile of mouldering scenery on the stage, has obtained permission to light his pipe, and is now practising swordsmanship at the expense of one of those contraptions of wire and padding upon the generous contours of which Victorian ladies were accustomed to create additions to their wardrobe. When he is not observing with satisfaction the easy havoc wrought upon this dummy, his eye follows Jay with considerable curiosity up and down the gallery. Lord Arthur Spendlove and Mr Armigel are amicably occupied in testing the strength of the pikes with which they have armed themselves. The more powerful moiety of Jay's juvenile army is at guard over the stair-head; the remainder are held in reserve upon the stage. Mrs Feather has the impression that she is the only person who is extremely frightened. She would like to lower the Titians on a cord through the window, call upon the criminals to take note and make off with them, and then herself pick up a couple of equivalent art treasures for Lord Scattergood on the open market. In all this Mrs Feather has not remotely in mind, indeed, either her own safety or her son's. But she is profoundly shocked that these children have already been involved in one scene of violence, and that they may presently be precipitated into another which may conceivably become a fight to the death. Mrs Feather is aware however that nobody is going to support her in this view, and that in their several ways all her companions are delivered over to a sort of mild madness. But if she is unable to prevent further hostilities it is incumbent upon her to prepare for them. She has had the foresight to raid a bedroom on her way to the gallery, and is in possession of a pair of linen sheets. With these she now retires to an unobtrusive corner and proceeds to the manufacture of bandages.

When the assault does come it is sudden and formidable. Grant, who is at the stair-head, is among the first to be aware of it. At one moment there is nothing below him but darkness and silence; at the next a powerful beam of light is sweeping up the staircase, and behind it, with a rush, come three or four men in a bunch. A bow twangs; there is a scream of pain; the powerful light vanishes; and in the same instant a lantern balanced on the barricade explodes in a shower of glass under the impact of a revolver bullet. Silence follows.

It must be said that the first round has been won. But the scream and the revolver-shot have done their work. In the uncertain light of lanterns, torches, and candles the adults look at the children, and then with fresh eyes at one another. In a voice that has held unquestioned authority in the western desert, Arthur Spendlove orders Jay's force to the far end of the gallery. Nobody moves. Jay's own brow is suddenly like thunder. It is decidedly a moment of crisis. Lord Scattergood, who appears to possess other than intellectual means of assessing and responding to a situation of this kind, leaps with surprising agility to the top of the barrier and down on the other side. 'This won't do,' he says. 'I shall go down and tell the blackguards what I think of them.' But he has not taken three steps before he is unexpectedly held up. A puff of acrid vapour comes up the staircase, and within a second it is a dense and stifling cloud. Lord Scattergood is driven back, blinded and coughing, over the barrier. There can be no question of what has happened. The enemy has let off some species of smoke screen with deadly effect. There is a great sound of breaking glass. Jay is smashing every window he can reach. Then there is a shrill whistle and his force is in tolerably orderly retreat to the east end of the gallery. As the adults, unpractised on this treacherous terrain, follow, the ancient flooring creaks dangerously beneath them.

And now the whole force is back on the little stage. Jay with astonishing rapidity orders individuals here and there. Already he has his best bowmen lurking in the canvas foliage of the wings or crouched behind the dusty burlap simulacra of gnarled logs and mossy banks. It is very much a last stand – and not in Arden but in Sherwood. The far end of the gallery is still obscured in smoke, but the stuff seems to be making no progress towards them. If the enemy is already established there he still has a daunting stretch of space to cover. Once more the defenders appear to have the upper hand. And suddenly Jay gives a shout. 'Listen!' He is echoed by a cry from the boy who is still at watch by a window. Faintly in the night can be heard a queer, distant ululation – a rising and falling note that it takes only a second to identify. A police-car, moving very fast on the high road, is taking no chances and freely sounding its siren.

Jay's army gives a yell of excitement. And at the same instant something fantastic begins to happen near the farther end of the gallery. The junk which lines its sides is moving. Old portmanteaux, mangles, cooking-stoves, chests are edging forward, while at the same time spreading across the floor. Behind this armour the enemy is advancing – cautiously but at a fair pace. It is taking no more chances with the bows of the defenders. Jay gives a sharp order, and a whole flight of arrows spends itself in vain. The advancing barrier is level with the Christmas box when something on the stage stirs, howls, leaps. The uncanny monster approaching has roused Lightning from his indifference at last; he takes one more leap and is on top of whatever it represents. There are shouts, cries, curses; and behind the barrier rise up the figures of several men, flailing with their arms as the wolf-hound attacks them. Two overbalance and collide; a heavy chest in the middle of the floor goes over with a crash; and suddenly the whole picture disappears inexplicably from view. Candleshoe shudders and sways through all its fabric, and its air is filled first with the crash of tumbling masonry and falling timbers and then with a dust so suffocating that it is impossible even to cry out at what has occurred. But there can be no doubt of the event. It is simple and definitive. The rotten and over-strained floor of the Long Gallery has given way throughout the greater part of its length. The criminals with much else have disappeared into the gulf with all the instantaneousness of a good *coup de théâtre*. Nothing much is left standing except the little stage – and upon it – incongruously – those who have been cast in the role of audience to this topsy-turvy drama.

The rumble of subsiding debris ceases and the air begins

to clear. Through the shattered windows men can be heard shouting – so many men as to put the sagacity of Robin's father beyond doubt. Grant has possessed himself of an electric torch, and with this he proceeds to make a survey of the position. At this east end of the gallery the beams and joists appear to have held, so that there seems no reason to fear a further collapse. The entire defending force is unscathed, and it should presently be possible to unblock the east staircase and descend.

Grant turns his torch upon the yawning cavity in the middle of the gallery and finds that the beam has no power to pierce its obscurity. It occurs to him that all the criminals may not have been engulfed; someone may have managed to scramble to the side. The beam reaches no more than half-way down the gallery; he plays it along first one wall and then the other. Some of the accumulated lumber has tumbled into the pit; some remains; there is no sign of a human form.

The beam halts. For a second Grant believes that he has spotted somebody after all – a single figure, standing pressed against the wall. Then he realizes that the figure is in marble; it is one of the youths who stands on either side of Gerard Christmas's monument. He moves the torch and sees that the corresponding figure is missing. The collapsing floor has carried with it part of the face of the monument. Where previously the marble curtains hung there is now vacancy. The torch probes this and uncertainly picks out a small chamber, once more piled with lumber, and thick with dust. Candleshoe has faced its crisis and the Christmas box has opened.

# CHAPTER TWENTY-ONE

THE ambulances have departed with the battered evil-doers, and Lightning is said to have enjoyed a large breakfast. Mrs Feather is glad of a cup of tea. The sunrise has struck her as particularly beautiful, and it is already warm on the terrace that flanks the eastern façade of Candleshoe Manor. The house has been sadly battered, but in this Mrs Feather sees a certain advantageousness. Major repairs being now essential, it should be possible to make a thorough job of restoration – including adequately modern domestic offices and first-class plumbing – without any risk of offending local or antiquarian sentiment.

And the rooms must be rearranged. With sudden inspiration, Mrs Feather sees that her breakfast-room should face this way. On a glorious summer morning such as this it will thus be possible for her guests to stroll out with their coffee to the terrace. For that matter, this is what everybody has done now; it is the presence of nearly all who have been concerned in the late untoward events, here assembled for the purpose of consuming whatever Tib, Jay, and Mr Armigel can provide, that has put this pleasant picture of future house-parties into Mrs Feather's head. And there is nobody here, she reflects, whom she would not much enjoy entertaining.

Except, conceivably, Dr Rosenwald. Perhaps it is because this eminent expert has only lately come into anybody's head, and been extracted in a thoroughly chilled condition from Lord Scattergood's car, that his disposition appears to Mrs Feather to be not of the first charm. The distinguished Roman, indeed, is concerned to make himself agreeable, and has already entered into conversation with Mrs Feather on the large opportunities that attend any American lady of conjoined means and taste who is minded to amass paintings under expert guidance.

Paintings, meanwhile, are occupying other members of the party. For it is paintings – all much browned and some of them sadly battered – that the Christmas box has proved chiefly to contain. This is an odd circumstance upon which Mr Archdeacon and Mr Armigel are even now in learned conference. They presently opine that Squire Candleshoe, at the time of his notable dispute with the first Earl of Scattergood, must have taken the precaution of stowing away in a secret chamber the access to which was still known to him such works of art as he had succeeded in abstracting from Solomon's Cottage. The librarian and the chaplain, armed with piles of dusters and assisted by Jay, turn over the oddly revealed little collection where it has been stacked at one end of the terrace, and presently they come upon what confirms their conjecture. This is a large canvas behind the accumulated dirt on which it is possible to discern what can only be an encounter of Actaeon and Diana.

'Ah – the Schiavone!' Mr Archdeacon is delighted. 'A most interesting minor painter of the Venetian School. Let us have Dr Rosenwald to confirm our discovery.'

Dr Rosenwald however, who conceives himself to be pressing home his advantage with Mrs Feather, declines for the moment to interest himself in such small game. Mr Archdeacon turns roguishly to his employer. 'Marquess, let us be quite clear about this, so that there may be no further dispute between the houses of Spendlove and Candleshoe. Miss Candleshoe has ceded you the Leda and the Lollia. Do you acknowledge that the Diana and Actaeon is hers?'

'Certainly, my dear Archdeacon. I can have no claim upon anything that has been come upon in this extraordinary way. And now bring Armigel here for a cup of this excellent tea.'

Jay is left, rather a lonely figure, turning over and dusting the remaining paintings. Grant Feather, watching him from a distance, sees that the contents of the Christmas box have been far from answering the boy's romantic expectations. Partly, perhaps, because the pirate hoard has revealed itself as no more than these dismal squares of darkened canvas, and partly as a reaction from his heroic defence of Candleshoe, Jay, for the first time in Grant's brief acquaintance with him, is visibly depressed. He examines the paintings one by one, conscientiously but listlessly. Then suddenly he pauses at his task. 'Grant,' he calls out, 'come here.'

Grant walks across the terrace. Jay is looking in some perplexity at the painting now beneath his hand. He has just wiped the dust from its surface, and what is revealed is the portrait of a youth, richly attired in what appears to be carnival costume, and holding in his hand a small black mask. Jay gives another wipe. 'I can't understand it,' he says. 'It looks familiar.'

Grant takes one glance and agrees. The portrait is clearly by an Italian painter of the early eighteenth century, and is of no high distinction. But it is extremely interesting, nevertheless. Jay may well find it perplexingly familiar. For the youth who looks squarely out of the canvas might be the mirror image of Jay Ray.

And suddenly, without a word from Grant, this comes to Jay. He turns even paler than usual, and then very quietly asks, 'Who is it?'

Everybody has gathered round. Jay turns from the portrait and looks at the circle of familiar faces with something like terror. Mr Armigel kneels down, adjusts his spectacles, and reads out an inscription. '*Johannes Candleshoe. Aet. Suae 19. Venezia 1720.* . . . This is undoubtedly a portrait of himself brought home by Jack Candleshoe from his Grand Tour.'

Miss Candleshoe has stepped forward. She takes one

look and speaks decisively. 'Then, pray, may I be told why this Jack Candleshoe is indistinguishable from Jay?'

'By all means.' Mr Archdeacon speaks from behind the first glorious cloud of tobacco smoke which he has allowed himself this morning. 'Jay is a Candleshoe. In fact, my dear madam, there can be little doubt that he is your heir.'

Rarely can it have fallen to a professional oracle – one with leisurely habits, metaphysical interests, and a highly involved and periphrastical form of address – to enjoy such an opportunity as is now Mr Archdeacon's. His explanations occupy just under an hour. And yet, in essence, they are extremely simple. He had, at the time of the depositing of the Benison pictures at Candleshoe, fallen into a relationship of some confidence and familiarity with the lately-established housekeeper, an American lady passing under the name of Mrs Ray. Perhaps because by that time Mr Archdeacon had already been in notable possession of the qualities of a sage, or perhaps simply because some confidant had become emotionally necessary to her, Mrs Ray had revealed that hers was a surprising and anomalous, yet wholly respectable situation. A Californian by birth, she had married, obscurely but with an undoubted legality, a shiftless Englishman named Rupert Candleshoe, who had very shortly thereafter died. The character of her husband having been far from such as to make her repose any ready confidence in his relations, and she herself being a woman of strong – even original – turn of mind, she had determined upon a little anonymous prospecting before entering into any overt connexion with them. This odd resolution it was that had brought her under her maiden name to Candleshoe; and at Candleshoe she had still been turning over her problem when she suddenly met with an accidental death. To Mr Archdeacon her conduct had appeared a shade fantastic. Yet this was perhaps essentially because he had remained without one vital piece of information. He had no notion that the lady passing as Mrs Ray had an infant child, or that the decision confronting her was whether her child's future should be that of an American lad with his own way to make, or that of a bankrupt English squire. Had Mr Archdeacon known of the orphaned Jay's existence, it would have been incumbent upon him to come forward with such facts as he knew. As it was, the strange situation apparently terminated by the lady's sudden death had seemed no affair of his, and the uncertain relationship always existing between Benison and Candleshoe had militated against any casual revelation. But the facts of the case were undoubted now; and Jay's mother in the course of her confidence had been sufficiently explicit in the matter of times and places to enable the situation to be investigated and corroborated by whatever legal personages would be concerned.

All this – which may have been felt by some as not altogether incongruously touched by the canons of eighteenth-century romance – is listened to with close attention by everybody on the terrace of Candleshoe. Or by everybody with one exception. Dr Rosenwald – understandably in view of his own just elevation above the vulgar concerns of common life – takes very little interest in the dénouement of our comedy. At first he sits in abstraction in the garden chair, presumably planning that campaign by which he will eventually secure for the happily-recovered Leda and Lollia a record price for Lord Scattergood and a record commission for himself. Then he gets up, prowls about, and presently takes a condescending look at the undistinguished treasure-trove which the Christmas box has afforded. He turns over the old neglected canvases, dusting his fingers gloomily between each. He arrives at the Diana and Actaeon, pauses on it, peers, scratches, peers again, and surprises the company by giving vent to a sudden loud cry.

'God bless my soul! I don't believe that fellow can be sober yet.' Lord Scattergood is apologetic. 'Arthur, do you think we could have Rosenwald taken away? I am afraid he has fallen into some sort of alcoholic delirium. It must have been all that whisky. Perhaps they don't drink it in Rome.'

'He certainly appears to be extremely excited.' Arthur Spendlove glances in perplexity at Dr Rosenwald, who is now waving his arms in what must be either mystical exaltation or agony.

Mr Archdeacon is also alarmed. 'His behaviour is certainly very aberrant. Would it, one wonders, be occasioned by a sudden abnegation of the ratiocinative faculty?'

'Off his rocker – eh?' Lord Scattergood is concerned. 'Oughtn't to have left him in that car all night. Delicate, no doubt – that sort.'

'It is, in my opinion, nothing less than possession.' Mr Armigel offers this. 'Mark – a sure sign of such a state – the confusion of tongues. Pandemonium, after all, is an international settlement.' Mr Armigel takes out his watch, glances at it, and walks away.

It is certainly true that a remarkable medley of the languages of Europe is tumbling from Dr Rosenwald's lips. But presently he controls himself sufficiently to point a trembling finger at the Diana and Actaeon, and to produce an approximation to intelligible sense. 'That ... that! It is whose ... what ... yes?'

'Whose, sir?' Miss Candleshoe is swift to have no doubts on this point. 'That painting, as you must yourself have heard Lord Scattergood acknowledge, is my property. Not, possibly, in an absolute sense. I am not altogether clear that it may not be entailed upon the issue of my late nephew – that is to say, upon Jay. It is Candleshoe property. Let that suffice.'

'And a Schiavone, you know.' Mr Archdeacon nods his head sagely. 'He is known to me as a painter of some little – '

'Schiavone!' Dr Rosenwald utters the name as a sort of howl in which are weirdly mingled derision, rage, and ecstasy. 'That painting is by Giorgione.'

'Is that so?' Lord Scattergood is a little crestfallen on Miss Candleshoe's behalf. 'But, my dear fellow, it should have some little value, all the same?'

This time Dr Rosenwald's howl is even more heavily loaded with conflicting emotions. Then, as with a supreme effort, he delivers himself tonelessly of two sentences. 'Giorgione is the greatest painter in the history of European art. And this will unquestionably be acknowledged as his greatest work.'

There is a blank silence. Jay, who has been sitting on the edge of the terrace staring deep into some world of his own, now turns round and addresses the Roman connoisseur gravely. 'The painting is worth a lot of money?'

'Yes, my child.'

'Enough to repair Candleshoe?'

Dr Rosenwald throws up his hands in disgust. 'It is worth more than any other painting in the world.' Then he brightens. 'Put it in my hands, and I will get you enough to build a Benison Court, if you want to.'

Jay rises. 'We shan't want to do that.' He brings his large watch from his pocket, looks at it, and then walks over to Miss Candleshoe. As he does so, from beyond the battered house, a cracked bell begins to sound. Miss Candleshoe hears it, bows majestically to Mrs Feather and the gentlemen assembled on the terrace, takes the arm of her young kinsman, and walks away.